Dean Koontz was born into a very poor family and learned early on to escape into fiction. Twenty-two of his novels have appeared in national and international bestseller lists and have sold over a hundred and twenty-five million copies worldwide.

He lives in southern California with his wife Gerda – and a vivid imagination.

Critical acclaim for

DARK RIVERS OF THE HEART

'The suspense is electrifying' *Publishers Weekly*

'Unrelenting excitement, truly memorable characters and ample food for thought launch this one to almost certain bestsellerdom' *Kirkus*

'Can only add to Dean's worldwide acclaim' *Today*

'Koontz's best book' *Time Out*

'Revelling equally in bad cons and good prose, Koontz gives a mindfreezing account of undercover government in the US' *Mail on Sunday*

MR MURDER

'Playing on every emotion and keeping the story racing along, Koontz masterfully escalates the tension. He closes the narrative with the most ingenious twist ending of his career' *Publishers Weekly*

'Koontz's art is making the reader believe the impossible . . . sit back and enjoy it' *Sunday Telegraph*

'Koontz whips up a tasty winter broth of peril and paranoia within the family' *Time Out*

Also by Dean Koontz

Fear Nothing
Demon Seed
Sole Survivor
Ticktock
Intensity
Strange Highways
Icebound
Dark Rivers of the Heart
Mr Murder
Dragon Tears
Hideaway
Cold Fire
The Bad Place
Midnight
Lightning
Watchers
Winter Moon
The Funhouse
The Mask
The Face of Fear
The Eyes of Darkness
The Door to December
The House of Thunder
The Key to Midnight
The Servants of Twilight
Shadowfires
Twilight Eyes
Darkness Comes
Night Chills
The Vision
The Voice of the Night
Strangers
Phantoms
Whispers
Shattered

Chase

Dean Koontz

**Previously published as
CHASE
by K R Dwyer**

Published in paperback in 1984 by Star Books
the paperback division of W H Allen & Co PLC

Reprinted in paperback in 1990
by HEADLINE BOOK PUBLISHING

Reprinted in this edition in 1995
by HEADLINE BOOK PUBLISHING

A HEADLINE FEATURE paperback

20 19 18 17 16 15 14 13

ISBN 0 7472 3525 2

Photoset by Intype, London
Printed and bound in Great Britain by
Clays Ltd, St Ives plc

HEADLINE BOOK PUBLISHING
A division of Hodder Headline PLC
338 Euston Road
London NW1 3BH

For Bob Hoskins

Preface to the New Version

Chase was my first suspense novel, written when I was a puppy. Although it was well reviewed upon publication, for years I yearned to revise it, because puppy work is never what it should have been. It is the nature of a writing career, however, that one is always plunging forward on new projects, drawn into new directions, and one seldom has the time to look back.

When a writer begins publishing as young as I was when I sold my first work, it is often a *good* idea never to look back, because the early books are to one degree or another as dubious as the offspring of a marriage between siblings. An opportunity arose for me to revise *Chase*, however, and I seized it. (How this came about is not quite as difficult to explain as is nuclear fusion but nearly so; consequently, I won't bore you with details.)

The character of Ben Chase still intrigues me,

and his story seems to me still to have power. In revising, I cut at least twenty-five percent of the original text, added new scenes, and undertook a complete cleanup of the prose and dialogue. As always happens when I revisit work from early in my career, I was tempted to change the entire intent of the story, the style, the plot, the characters – and turn it into a piece that would read exactly as if I had written it today. That isn't the point of revising older work, of course; rather, one should preserve the essence of what was there while making the experience of the book more effective for the reader. I restrained myself. I allowed Ben Chase to live the adventure he lived previously – but more concisely and with more point.

Chase is straight psychological suspense, with no hint of the supernatural. It's also character driven, relying almost entirely on the character of Benjamin Chase for its effect, so if he doesn't intrigue you, I'm in deep trouble. One additional warning: This is a rather dark piece, and some of Ben Chase's moral choices may startle you, Gentle Reader – though they are virtually the only ones that he could have made.

– Dean Koontz, 1995

Chase

1

1971.

Bruce Springsteen wasn't famous in 1971. Neither was Tom Cruise, a mere schoolboy. Julia Roberts haunted no young men's dreams. Robin Williams, Steve Martin, Arnold Schwarzenegger – their fortunes were as yet unmade.

Richard Milhous Nixon was President of the United States. The war in Vietnam raged. In Wilmington, North Carolina, January was a time of violence against black citizens – arson, bombings, shootings. At the Attica Correctional Facility in New York State, the bloodiest prison riot in U.S. history claimed forty-three lives.

The best-seller list of *The New York Times* included *The Winds of War* by Herman Wouk and *Another Roadside Attraction* by Tom Robbins.

The movies: *The French Connection, A Clockwork Orange, Klute, Carnal Knowledge, The Last Picture Show.*

The music: Carole King, John Denver, John Lennon on his own, Led Zeppelin, Elton John just beginning.

Cigarette sales in the United States topped five hundred and forty-seven *billion*. J. C. Penney died at the age of ninety-five. As many as five hundred thousand Soviet citizens perished in the Gulags during those twelve months – evidence of government restraint.

It was a different time. A different world.

The term 'serial killer' was unknown. And 'sociopath.'

2

At seven o'clock, seated on the platform as the guest of honor, Ben Chase was served a bad roast-beef dinner while dignitaries talked at him from both sides, breathing over his salad and his half-eaten fruit cup.

At eight o'clock the mayor rose to deliver a boring panegyric to the city's most famous Vietnam War hero. Half an hour after he began, he finally presented Chase with a special scroll detailing his supposed accomplishments and restating the city's pride in him.

Chase was also given the keys to a new Mustang convertible, which he had not been expecting. It was a gift from the Merchants' Association.

By nine-thirty Benjamin Chase was escorted from the Iron Kettle Restaurant to the parking lot where his new car waited. It was an eight-cylinder job with a sports package that included automatic transmission with a floor shift, bucket seats, side mirrors, white-wall tires – and a wickedly sparkling black paint job that contrasted nicely with the crimson racing stripes over the trunk and hood.

At ten minutes after ten, having posed for newspaper photographs with the mayor and the officers of the Merchants' Association, having expressed his gratitude to everyone present, Chase drove away in his reward.

At twenty minutes past ten he passed through the suburban development known as Ashside, doing slightly more than one hundred miles an hour in a forty-mile-an-hour zone. He crossed three-lane Galasio Boulevard against the light, turned a corner at such speed that he briefly lost control, and sheared off a traffic sign.

At ten-thirty he started up the long slope of Kanackaway Ridge Road, trying to see if he could hold the speed at one hundred all the way to the summit. It was a dangerous bit of play, but he did not care if he killed himself.

Perhaps because the car had not yet been broken in, or perhaps because it simply had not been designed for that kind of driving, it wouldn't perform as he wished. Although he held the accelerator to the floor, the speedometer registered only eighty miles per hour by the time that he was two thirds of the way up the winding

4

road; it fell to seventy when he crested the rise.

He took his foot off the accelerator – the fire of anger having burned out of him for the moment – and let the sleek machine glide along the flat stretch of two-lane blacktop along the ridge above the city.

Below lay a panorama of lights to stir the hearts of lovers. Though the left side of the road lay against a sheer rock wall, the right was maintained as a park. Fifty yards of grassy verge, dotted with shrubs, separated the street from an iron and concrete railing near the brink of the cliff. Beyond the railing, the streets of the city far below seemed like a miniature electric map, with special concentrations of light toward the downtown area and out near the Gateway Mall shopping center.

Lovers, mostly teenagers, parked here, separated by stands of pine and rows of brambles. Their appreciation for the dazzling city view turned – in almost every case and dozens of times each night – to an appreciation of the flesh.

Once, it had even been that way for Chase.

He pulled the car to the shoulder of the road, braked, and cut the engine. The stillness of the night seemed complete and deep. Then he heard crickets, the cry of an owl somewhere close, and the occasional laughter of young people muffled by closed car windows.

Until he heard the laughter, it did not occur to Chase to wonder why he had come here. He felt oppressed by the mayor, the Merchants' Association, and the rest of them. He had not really wanted the banquet, certainly not the car, and he had gone only because he could find no gracious way to decline them. Confronted with their homespun patriotism and their sugar-glazed vision of the war, he felt burdened with an indefinable load, smothered. Perhaps it was the past on his shoulders – the realization that he'd once shared their innocence. At any rate, free of them, he had struck out for that one place in the city that represented remembered pleasure, the much-joked-about lovers' lane atop Kanackaway.

Now, however, the comparative silence only gave his thoughts a chance to build toward a scream. And the pleasure? None of that, either, for he had no girl with him – and would have been no better off with one at his side.

Along the shadowed length of the park, half a dozen cars were slotted against walls of shrubbery. Moonlight glinted on the bumpers and windows. If he had not known the purpose of this retreat, he would have thought that all the vehicles were abandoned. But the mist on the inside of the windows gave the game away.

Occasionally a shadow moved inside one of the

cars, distorted by the steamed glass. Those sil-
houettes and the rustle of leaves as the wind
swept down from the top of the ridge were all
that moved.

Then something dropped from a low point on
the rock wall to the left and scurried across the
blacktop toward the darkness beneath a huge
weeping willow tree a hundred feet in front of
Chase's car. Though bent and moving with the
frantic grace of a frightened animal, the new
arrival was clearly a man.

In Vietnam, Chase had developed an uncanny
sense of imminent danger. His inner alarm was
clanging.

The one thing that did not belong in a lovers'
lane at night was a man alone, on foot. A teenager's car was a mobile bed, such a necessity of
seduction, such an extension of the seducer, that
no modern Casanova could be successful without
one.

It was possible, of course, that the interloper
was engaging in some bird-dogging: spotting parkers for his own amusement and to their embarrassment. Chase had been the victim of that
game a few times in his high-school years. That
was, however, a pastime usually associated with
the immature or the socially outcast, those kids
who hadn't the opportunity to be *inside* the cars
where the real action was. It was not, as far as

Chase knew, something that adults enjoyed. And this man creeping through the shadows was easily six feet tall; he had the carriage of an adult, no youthful awkwardness. Besides, bird-dogging was a sport most often played in groups as protection against a beating from one of the surprised lovers.

Trouble.

The guy came out from beneath the willow, still doubled over and running. He stopped against a bramble row and studied a three-year-old Chevrolet parked at the end, near the cliff railing.

Not sure what was happening or what he should do, Chase turned in his car seat and worked the cover off the dome light. He unscrewed the tiny bulb and dropped it into a pocket of his suit jacket. When he turned front again, he saw that the bird-dogger had not moved: The guy was still watching the Chevrolet, leaning into the brambles as if unfazed by the thorns.

A girl laughed, the sound of her voice clear in the night air. Some of the lovers must have found it too warm for closed windows.

The man by the brambles moved again, closing on the Chevrolet.

Quietly, because the stalker was no more than a hundred and fifty feet from him, Chase got out of the Mustang. He left the door open, because he was sure that the sound of it would alert the intruder. He went around the car and across the grass, which had recently been mown and was slightly damp and slippery underfoot.

Ahead, a light came on in the Chevrolet, diffused by the steamed windows. Someone shouted, and a young girl screamed. She screamed again.

Chase had been walking. Now he ran as the sounds of a fight rose ahead. When he came up on the Chevrolet, he saw that the door on the driver's side was open and that the intruder was halfway into the front seat, flailing away at someone. Shadows bobbled, dipped, and pitched against the frosted glass.

'Hold it!' Chase shouted, directly behind the man now.

As the stranger pulled back out of the car, Chase saw the knife. The bird-dogger held it in his right hand, raised high. His hand and the weapon were covered with blood.

Chase raced forward the last few feet, slammed the stalker against the Chevy's window post. He slipped his arm around the guy's neck and tried to get a hammerlock on him.

The girl was still screaming.

The stranger swung his arm down and back, trying to catch Chase's thigh with the blade. He was an amateur.

Chase twisted out of the arc of the weapon.

Simultaneously he drew his arm more tightly across the other's windpipe.

Around them, cars started. Trouble in lovers' lane aroused all the repressed sexual guilt in every teenager nearby. No one wanted to stay to see what the problem was.

'Drop it,' Chase said.

Although the stranger must have been desperate for breath, he stabbed backward again and missed again.

Suddenly furious, Chase jerked his adversary onto his toes and applied the last effort necessary to choke him unconscious.

In the same instant, the wet grass betrayed him. His feet slipped, and he went down with the stranger on top.

This time the knife took Chase in the meaty part of his thigh, just below the hip. But it was torn from the assailant's hand as Chase bucked and tossed him aside.

The stalker rolled and scrambled to his feet. He took a few steps toward Chase, seeking the knife, but then he seemed to realize the formidable nature of his opponent. He ran.

'Stop him!' Chase shouted.

But most of the cars had gone. Those still parked along the cliff reacted to this latest uproar just as the more timid parkers had reacted to the first cries: lights flickered on, engines started, tires squealed. In a moment the only cars in lovers' lane were the Chevrolet and Chase's Mustang.

The pain in his leg was bad, though not any worse than a hundred others he had endured. In the light from the Chevrolet, he could see that he was bleeding slowly from a shallow wound – not the fearsome spurt of a torn artery. When he tried, he was able to stand and walk with little trouble.

He went to the car, peered in, and then wished that he hadn't been curious. The body of a young man, perhaps nineteen or twenty, was sprawled half on the seat and half on the floor. Blood-soaked. Mouth open. Eyes glazed.

Beyond the victim, curled in the corner by the far door, a petite brunette, a year or two younger than her murdered lover, was moaning softly. Her hands gripped her knees so tightly that they resembled claws latched around a piece of game. She wore a pink miniskirt but no blouse or bra. Her small breasts were spotted with blood, and her nipples were erect.

Chase wondered why this last detail registered more vividly with him than anything else about the grisly scene.

He expected better of himself. Or at least – there had been a time when he had expected better.

11

'Stay there,' Chase said from the driver's door. 'I'll come around for you.'

She did not respond, though she continued to moan.

Chase almost closed the door, then realized that he would be shutting off the light and leaving the brunette alone in the car with the corpse. He walked around the Chevy, leaning on it to favor his right leg, and he opened her door.

Apparently these kids had not believed in locks. That was, he supposed, part of their generation's optimism, part and parcel with their theories on free love, mutual trust, and brotherhood. Theirs was the same generation that was supposed to live life so fully that they all but denied the existence of death.

Their generation. Chase was only a few years older than they were. But he did not consider himself to be part of their generation or any other. He was alone in the flow of time.

'Where's your blouse?' he asked.

She was no longer fixated on the corpse, but she was not looking at Chase either. She stared at her knees, at her white knuckles, and she mumbled.

Chase groped around on the floor under her legs and found the balled-up garment. 'You better put this on.'

She wouldn't take it. She continued murmuring wordlessly to herself.

'Come on, now,' he said as gently as he could.

The killer might not have gone very far.

She spoke more urgently now, coherently, although her voice was lower than before. When he bent closer to listen, he discovered that she was saying, 'Please don't hurt me, please don't hurt me.'

'I won't hurt you,' Chase assured her, straightening up. 'I didn't do that to your boyfriend. But the man who did it might still be hanging around. My car's back there. Will you please come with me?'

She blinked, nodded, and got out of the car. He handed the blouse to her. She unrolled it, shook it out, but could not seem to get it on. She was still in a state of shock.

'You can dress in my car,' Chase said. 'It's safer there.'

The shadows under the trees were deeper than they had been.

He put his arm around her and half carried her back to the Mustang. The door on the passenger's side was locked. By the time he got her to the other door and followed her inside, she seemed to have recovered her senses. She slipped one arm into the blouse, then the other, and slowly buttoned it.

When he closed his door and started the engine, she said, 'Who are you?'

13

'Passerby. I saw the bastard and thought something was wrong.'

'He killed Mike,' she said hollowly.

'Your boyfriend?'

She didn't respond but leaned back against the seat, chewing her lip and wiping absentmindedly at the few spots of blood on her face.

'We'll get to a phone – or a police station. You all right? You need a hospital?'

'No.'

Chase swung the car around and drove down Kanackaway Ridge Road as fast as he had driven up. He took the turn at the bottom so hard that the girl was thrown against the door.

'Buckle your seat belt,' he advised.

She did as directed, but she appeared to be in a daze, staring straight ahead at the streets that unrolled before them.

'Who was he?' Chase asked as he reached the intersection at Galasio Boulevard and crossed it with the light this time.

'Mike,' she said.

'Not your boyfriend.'

'What?'

'The other one.'

'I don't know,' she said.

'Did you see his face?'

She frowned. 'His face?'

'Yes.'

14

'Face.' As if the word were meaningless to her.
'Have you been doing anything?' he asked.
'Anything?'
'Drugs?'
'A little grass. Earlier.'
Maybe more than a little, he decided.
He tried again: 'Did you see his face? Did you recognize him?'
'Face? No. Yes. Not really. A little.'
'I thought it might be an old lover, rejected suitor, something like that.'
She said nothing.
Her reluctance to talk about it gave Chase time to consider the situation. As he recalled the killer's approach from the top of the ridge, he began to wonder whether the man had known which car he was after or whether any car would have done, whether this was an act of revenge directed against Mike specifically or only the work of a madman. Even before he had been sent overseas, the papers had been filled with stories of meaningless slaughter. He had not read any papers since his discharge, but he suspected that the same brand of senseless murder still flourished.
The possibility of random, unmotivated homicide unnerved him. The similarity to Nam, to Operation Jules Verne and his part in it, stirred bad memories.

15

Fifteen minutes after they had left the ridge, Chase parked in front of the divisional police headquarters on Kensington Avenue.

'Are you feeling well enough to talk with them?' Chase asked.

'Cops?'

'Yeah.'

She shrugged. 'I guess so.'

She had recovered remarkably fast. She even had the presence of mind to take Chase's pocket comb and run it through her dark hair. 'How do I look?'

'Fine.'

Maybe it was better to be without a woman than to die and leave behind one who grieved so briefly as this.

'Let's go,' she said. She opened her door and stepped out, her lovely, trim legs flashing in a rustle of brief cloth.

* * *

The door of the small gray room opened, admitting a small gray man. His face was lined, and his eyes were sunken as if he had not slept in a day or two. His light-brown hair was uncombed and in need of a trim. He crossed to the table behind which Chase and the girl sat, and he took the only chair left. He folded into it as if he

16

would never get up again. 'I'm Detective Wallace.'

'Glad to meet you,' Chase said, though he was not glad at all.

The girl was quiet, examining her nails.

'Now, what's this all about?' Wallace asked, folding his hands on the scarred table and regarding them wearily, as if he'd already heard their story countless times.

'I already told the desk sergeant most of it,' Chase said.

'He isn't in homicide. I am,' Wallace said.

'Someone should be on the way out there. The body – '

'A car's been despatched. Your report's being checked out. That's what we do. Maybe not always well, but we do it. So you say someone was murdered.'

'Her boyfriend, stabbed,' Chase told him.

Wallace studied the girl as she studied her nails. 'Can't she speak?'

'She's in shock maybe.'

'These days?' Wallace joked, exhibiting a disregard for the girl's feelings that Chase found disconcerting.

The girl said, 'Yeah, I can speak.'

'What's your name?' Wallace asked.

'Louise.'

'Louise what?'

'Allenby. Louise Allenby.'

Wallace said, 'You live in the city?'

'In Ashside.'

'How old?'

Anger flared in her, but then she damped it and turned her gaze back to her nails. 'Seventeen.'

'In high school?'

'I graduated in June,' she said. 'I'm going to college in the fall. Penn State.'

Wallace said, 'Who was the boy?'

'Mike.'

'That's it?'

'That's what?'

'Just Mike? Like Liberace. Like Picasso? One name?'

'Michael Karnes,' she said.

'Just a boyfriend, or you engaged?'

'Boyfriend. We'd been going together for about a year, kind of steady.'

'What were you doing on Kanackaway Ridge Road?' Wallace asked.

She looked boldly at him. 'What do you think?'

Though Wallace's bored tone was disconcerting, Chase found the girl's detachment so unnerving that he wanted to be away from her as quickly as possible. 'Look, Detective Wallace,' he interjected, 'is this really necessary? The girl wasn't involved in it. I think the guy might've gone for her next if I hadn't stopped him.'

Wallace said, 'How'd you happen to be there in the first place?'

'Just out driving,' Chase said.

A light of interest switched on in the detective's eyes. 'What's your name?'

'Benjamin Chase.'

'I *thought* I'd seen you before.' His manner softened and his energy level rose. 'Your picture was in the papers today.'

Chase nodded.

'That was really something you did over there,' Wallace said. 'That really took guts.'

'It wasn't as much as they make out,' Chase said.

'I'll *bet* it wasn't!' Wallace said, though it was clear that he thought Chase's actions in Vietnam must have been even more heroic than the papers had portrayed them.

The girl had taken a new interest in Chase and was studying him openly.

Wallace's tone toward her changed too. He said, 'You want to tell me about it, just how it happened?'

She told him, losing some of her eerie composure in the process. Twice Chase thought that she was going to cry, and he wished that she would. Her cold manner, so soon after all the blood, gave him the creeps. Maybe she *was* still in denial. She repressed the tears, and by the time she had finished her story, she was calm again.

'You saw his face?' Wallace asked.

'Just a glimpse,' she said.

'Can you describe him?'

'Not really.'

'Try.'

'He had brown eyes, I think.'

'No mustache or beard?'

'I don't think so.'

'Long sideburns or short?'

'Short, I think.'

'Any scars?'

'No.'

'Anything at all memorable about him?

'No.'

'The shape of his face – '

'No.'

'No what?'

'It was just a face, any shape.'

'His hair receding or full?'

'I can't remember,' she said.

Chase said, 'When I got to her, she was in a state of shock. I doubt she was registering anything.'

Instead of a grateful agreement, Louise scowled at him.

He realized, too late, that the worst embarrassment for someone Louise's age was to lose her cool, to fail to cope. He had betrayed her momentary lapse to, of all people, a cop. She would have little gratitude for him now, even though he had saved her life.

Wallace got up. 'Come on,' he said.

'Where?' Chase asked.

'We'll go out there.'

'Is that really necessary? For me, anyway?' Chase asked.

'Well, I have to take statements from both of you, in more detail than this. It would help, Mr. Chase, to be on the scene when you're describing it again. It'll only take a short while. We'll need the girl longer than we'll need you.'

* * *

Chase was sitting in the rear of Wallace's squad car, thirty feet from the scene of the murder, answering questions, when the staff car from the *Press-Dispatch* arrived. Two photographers and a reporter got out.

For the first time, Chase realized that there would be local newspaper and television coverage. They would make a reluctant hero of him. Again.

'Please,' he said to Wallace, 'can we keep the reporters from learning who helped the girl?'

'Why?'

'I'm tired of reporters,' Chase said.

Wallace said, 'But you did save her life. You ought to be proud of that.'

'I don't want to talk to them,' Chase said.

'That's up to you. But they'll have to know who interrupted the killer. It'll be in the report.'

Later, when Wallace was finished and Chase was getting out of the car to join another officer who would take him back to town, he felt the girl put a hand on his shoulder. He turned, and she said, 'Thank you.'

Maybe he was imagining it, but he thought that her touch had the quality of a caress and that her hand lingered. Even the possibility sickened him.

He met her eyes. Looked away at once.

At the same instant, a photographer snapped a picture. The flashbulb sprayed light. The light was brief – but the photograph would haunt him forever.

In the car, on the way back to town, the uniformed officer behind the wheel said that his name was Don Jones, that he had read about Chase, and that he would like to have Chase's autograph for his kids. Chase signed his name on the back of a blank homicide report, and at Jones's urging, he prefaced it with 'To Rick and Judy Jones.' The officer asked a lot of questions about Nam, which Chase answered as curtly as courtesy would allow.

In his prize Mustang, he drove more sedately than he had before. There was no anger in him now, only infinite weariness.

At a quarter past one in the morning, he parked in front of Mrs. Fielding's house, relieved to see that no lights were on. He unlocked the front door as quietly as the ancient deadbolt would permit, stepped knowingly around most of the loose boards in the staircase, and made his way to his attic apartment: one large room that served as a kitchen, bedroom, and living room, plus one walk-in closet and a private bath.

He locked his door.

He felt safe now.

Of course, he knew that he would never be safe again. No one ever was. Safety was an illusion.

This night at least, he hadn't been required to make polite conversation with Mrs. Fielding as she posed coyly in one of her half-unbuttoned housedresses, revealing the fish-belly-white curves of her breasts. He never understood why she chose to be so casually immodest at her age.

He undressed. He washed his face and hands. In fact, he washed his hands three times. He washed his hands a lot lately.

He studied the shallow knife wound in his thigh. It was already clotted and beginning to scab. He washed it, flushed it with alcohol, swabbed it with Merthiolate, and bandaged it.

In the main room, he completed the medication

by pouring a glass of Jack Daniel's over two ice cubes. He sank onto the bed with the whiskey. He usually consumed half a bottle a day, minimum. This day, because of the damn banquet, he'd tried to stay sober. No longer.

Drinking, he felt clean again. Alone with a bottle of good liquor – that was the *only* time he felt clean.

He was pouring his second glassful when the telephone rang.

When he had first moved into the apartment, he hadn't wanted a telephone. No one would ever call. And he had no desire to make contact with anyone.

Mrs. Fielding had not believed that he could live without a phone. Envisioning herself becoming a messenger service for him, she had insisted that he have a telephone hooked up as a condition of occupancy.

That had been long before she knew that he was a war hero. It was even before *he* knew it.

For months the phone went unused except when she called from downstairs to tell him that mail had been delivered or to invite him to dinner.

Since the announcement by the White House, however, since all the excitement about the medal, he received calls every day, most of them from perfect strangers who offered congratu-

lations that he did not deserve or sought interviews for publications that he had never read.
He cut most of them short. Thus far, no one had
ever had gall enough to ring him up this late at
night, but he supposed he could never regain the
solitude to which he had grown accustomed in
those first months after his discharge.

He considered ignoring the phone and concen-
trating on his Jack Daniel's. But when it had
rung for the sixteenth time, he realized that the
caller was too persistent to be ignored, and he
answered it. 'Hello?'

'Chase?'

'Yes.'

'Do you know me?'

'No,' he said, unable to place the voice. The
man sounded tired – but aside from that one
clue, he might have been anywhere between
twenty and sixty years old, fat or thin, tall or
short.

'How's your leg, Chase?' His voice contained a
hint of humor, though the reason for it escaped
Chase.

'Good enough,' Chase said. 'Fine.'

'You're very good with your hands.'

Chase said nothing, could not bring himself to
speak, for now he understood what the call was
about.

'Very good with your hands,' the bird-dogger

repeated. 'I guess you learned that in the army.'

'Yes,' Chase said.

'I guess you learned a lot of things in the army, and I guess you think you can take care of yourself pretty well.'

Chase said, 'Is this *you?*'

The man laughed, momentarily shaking off his dispirited tone. 'Yes, it's me. I am me. Exactly right. I've got a badly bruised throat, Chase, and I know my voice will be just awful by morning. Otherwise, I got away about as lightly as you did.'

With a clarity reserved for moments of danger, Chase recalled the struggle with the killer on the grass by the Chevrolet. He tried to get a clear picture of the man's face but could do no better for his own sake than he had for the police. 'How did you know I was the one who stopped you?'

'I saw your picture in the paper. You're a war hero. Your picture was everywhere. When you were lying on your back, beside the knife, I recognized you and got out of there fast.'

'Who are you?'

'Do you really expect me to say?'

Chase had forgotten his drink altogether. The alarms, the goddamn alarms in his head, were ringing at peak volume. 'What do you want?'

The stranger was silent for so long that Chase almost asked the question again. Suddenly, the amusement gone from his voice, the killer said, 'You messed in where you had no right messing. You don't know the trouble I went to, picking the proper targets out of all those young fornicators, the ones who most deserved to die. I planned it for weeks, Chase, and I had given that young sinner his just punishment. The slut was left, and you saved her before I could perform my duty, saved a whore like that who had no right to be spared. This is not a good thing.'

'You're not well.' Chase realized the absurd inadequacy of that statement, but the killer – like all else in the modern world – had reduced him to cliches.

The killer either did not hear or pretended not to hear what Chase had said. 'I just wanted to tell you, Mr. Chase, that it doesn't end here. You are not a facilitator of justice.'

'What do you mean?'

'I'll deal with you, Chase, once I've researched your background and have weighed a proper judgment on you. Then, when you've been made to pay, I'll deal with the whore, that girl.'

'Deal with?' Chase asked.

The euphemism reminded him of the similar evasions of vocabulary to which he had grown accustomed in Nam. He felt much older than he was, more tired than he had been a moment earlier.

'I'm going to kill you, Chase. I'm going to

punish you for whatever sins are on your record, because you've interfered with the intended pattern. You are not a facilitator of justice.' He was silent. Then: 'Do you understand?'

'As much as I understand anything.'

'That's all you have to say?'

'What more?' Chase wondered.

'I'll be talking to you again.'

'What's the point of this?'

'Facilitation,' the killer said – and disconnected.

Chase hung up and leaned back against the headboard of the bed. He felt something cold in his hand, looked down, and was surprised to see the glass of whiskey. He raised it to his lips and took a taste. It was slightly bitter.

He closed his eyes.

So easy not to care.

Or maybe not so easy. If it had been as easy as he wanted it to be, he could have put the whiskey aside and gone to sleep. Or, instead of waiting for the bird-dogger to come after him, he could have blown out his own brains.

Too easy to care. He opened his eyes.

He had to decide what to do about the call.

The police would be interested, of course, because it was a solid lead to the man who had killed Michael Karnes. They would probably want to monitor the telephone line in hope that the killer would call again — especially since he had said that Chase would be hearing from him. They might even station an officer in Chase's room, and they might put a tail on him both for his own protection and to try to nab the murderer.

Yet he hesitated to call Detective Wallace.

The past few weeks, since the news about the Medal of Honor, Chase's daily routine had been destroyed. He loathed the change.

He had been accustomed to deep solitude, disturbed only by his need to talk to store clerks and to Mrs. Fielding, his landlady. In the mornings he went downtown and had breakfast at Woolworth's. He bought a paperback, occasionally a magazine — but never a newspaper — picked up what incidentals he required, stopped twice a week at the liquor store, spent the noon hour in the park watching the girls in their short skirts as they walked to and from their jobs, then went home and passed the rest of the day in his room. He read during the long afternoons, and he drank. By evening he could not clearly see the print on the pages of his book, and he turned on the small television to watch old movies that he had memorized virtually scene by scene. Around eleven o'clock, he finished the day's bottle or portion thereof, after having eaten little or nothing for dinner – and then he slept as long as he could.

It was not much of a life, certainly not what he had once expected, but it was bearable. Because it was simple, it was also solid, safe, empty of doubt and uncertainty, lacking in choices and decisions that might bring about another breakdown.

Then, after the AP and UPI carried the story of the Vietnam hero who had declined to attend a White House ceremony for the awarding of the Congressional Medal of Honor (though he had not declined the medal itself, since he felt that would bring more publicity than he could handle), there had been no hope of simplicity.

He had weathered the uproar, granting as few interviews as possible, talking in monosyllables on the phone. The only thing for which he had been required to leave his room was the banquet, and he had been able to cope with that only because he knew that once it was over, he could return to his attic apartment and resume the uneventful life that had been wrenched from him.

The incident in lovers' lane had changed his plans, postponed a return to stability. The papers would carry the Medal of Honor story again, with pictures, along with the report of his latest act of foolish interference. There would be more calls, congratulations, interviewers to be turned down.

Then it would die out. In a week or two – if he could tolerate the spotlight that long – things would be as they had once been, quiet and manageable.

He took another swallow of whiskey. It tasted better than it had a short while ago.

There were limits to what he could endure. Two more weeks of newspaper stories, phone calls, job offers, and marriage proposals would take him to the end of his meager resources. During that same time, if he had to share his room with an officer of the law and be followed everywhere he went, he would not hold up.

Already he felt the same vague emptiness arising in him that had filled him so completely in the hospital. It was that profound lack of purpose that he must stave off at all costs. Even if it meant withholding information from the authorities.

He wouldn't tell the police about the call.

He drank more Jack Daniel's.

Good people down there in Tennessee, distilling Jack Daniel's for the solace of the world. Good product. Better than fame or praise or love. And cheaper.

He went to the cupboard and refreshed the glass with another two ounces from the dark bottle.

He worried that he was keeping a lead from the police, but the cops were clever. They would find the man without Chase's assistance. They would find fingerprints on the door handle of the Chevrolet and on the murder weapon. He knew that they had already issued a statement to the effect that the killer would be suffering from a badly bruised throat and resultant laryngitis.

What Chase was keeping from them would do little to speed up their efficient law-enforcement machine.

He knew he was lying to himself.

It wasn't the first time.

He finished his drink. It went down quickly, smoothly.

He poured more whiskey, returned to bed, slid beneath the covers, and stared at the blank eye of the television.

In a few days everything would be back to normal. As normal as this world could ever be. He could settle into old routines, living comfortably on his disability pension and the moderate inheritance from his parents' estate.

He had no need to get a job or to talk to anyone or to make decisions. His only task was to consume enough whiskey to be able to sleep despite the nightmares.

He wasn't lonely: He communed with Jack Daniel's.

He watched the blank television.

Sometimes he felt that the TV was watching him too.

Time passed. It always did.

He slept.

3

Chase rose early the next morning, frightened awake by dead men talking to him through mouths full of graveyard soil. After that the day deteriorated.

His mistake was in trying to go on with his day as if the events of the previous night had never happened. He rose, bathed, shaved, dressed, and went downstairs to see if there was any mail on the hall table. There was none, but Mrs. Fielding heard him and hurried out of the perpetually gloomy living room to show him the first edition of the *Press-Dispatch*. His picture was on the front page: He was turning toward Louise Allenby as she got out of a squad car. The girl appeared to be crying, gripping his arm with one hand, looking far more grief stricken than she had actually been.

'I'm so proud of you,' Mrs. Fielding said.

She sounded as though she were his mother.

Indeed, she was old enough for the post – though whatever mothering instinct she showed always seemed strained and false. Her hair was tightly curled and bleached blond. The excessive rouge and bright lipstick made her seem older than she actually was.

'It wasn't anything like they said, not as exciting as that,' Chase told her.

'How do you know? You haven't read it.'

'They always exaggerate. Reporters.'

'Oh, you're just too modest,' Mrs. Fielding said.

She was wearing a blue and yellow housedress with the two top buttons undone. Chase could see the pallid bulge of her breasts and the edge of a lacy yellow brassiere.

Though he was much stronger and much younger than Mrs. Fielding, she frightened him. Perhaps because he could not figure out what she wanted from him.

She seemed to want something more than the rent. More than some companionship. There was a desperation in her – maybe because she herself didn't know what she wanted.

She said, 'I bet this brings twice the job offers that the last article brought!'

Mrs. Fielding was much more interested in Chase's eventual employment than was Chase himself. At first he'd thought that she was afraid he would fall in arrears on the rent, but he'd eventually decided that her concern went deeper than that.

She said, 'As I've often told you, you're young and strong, and you have a lifetime ahead of you. The thing for a fellow like you is work, hard work, a chance to make something of yourself. Not that you haven't done all right so far. Don't misunderstand me. But this lounging around, not working – it hasn't been good for you. You must have lost fifteen pounds since you first moved in.'

Chase did not respond.

Mrs. Fielding moved closer to him and took the morning paper out of his hands. She stared at the picture in the center of the front page and sighed.

'I have to be going,' Chase said.

She looked up from the paper. 'I *saw* your car.'

'Yes.'

'Do you like it?'

'It's a car.'

'It tells about the car in the paper.'

'I suppose it docs.'

'Wasn't that nice of them?'

'Yes. Very nice.'

'They hardly ever do anything for the boys who serve and don't make a big protest of it. You read all about the bad ones, but no one ever lifts a hand for good boys like you. It's about time, and I hope you enjoy the car.'

'Thank you,' he said, opening the front door and stepping outside, trying not to look as though he were fleeing.

He drove to Woolworth's for breakfast.

The novelty of the car had worn off. He would have preferred to walk. There were too many decisions to make while driving a car. Walking was simpler. Walking, it was easier to shut the mind off and just drift along.

Ordinarily, the lunch counter at Woolworth's was a guarantee of privacy, even when every stool was taken. Businessmen reading the financial pages, secretaries drinking coffee and doing crossword puzzles, laborers hunched over plates of eggs and bacon – all wanted a moment of solitude before the daily hubbub began. Strangely, the elbow-to-elbow proximity fostered a respect for privacy. That Tuesday morning, however, halfway through his meal, Chase discovered that most of the other customers were watching him with only poorly disguised interest.

The ubiquitous newspaper with the front-page photograph had betrayed him.

He stopped eating, left a tip, paid his check, and got out of there. His hands were shaking, and the backs of his knees quivered as if his legs would fail him.

He didn't like being watched. He didn't even like being smiled at by a waitress or a clerk. His preference was to go through life as one of those nondescript men whom people looked *through*.

When he went to the newsstand around the corner from Woolworth's to purchase a paperback, he was confronted with so many images of his face in the newspaper racks that he turned away at the door without going in.

At the nearby liquor store, for the first time in months, the clerk commented on the size of the whiskey purchase. Clearly, he felt that a man like Chase shouldn't be buying so much booze. Unless, of course, the whiskey was for a party.

'Giving a party?' the clerk asked.

'Yeah.'

Anxious for the barren confines of his little attic room, Chase walked two blocks toward home before he remembered that he now owned a car. He walked back to it, embarrassed that someone might have seen his confusion.

When he settled behind the wheel, he felt too tightly wound to risk driving. He sat for fifteen minutes, paging through the service manual and the ownership papers before finally starting the engine and pulling away from the curb.

He didn't go to the park to watch the girls on their lunch hour, because he feared recognition. If someone tried to strike up a conversation, he would not know what to say.

In his room, he poured a glass of whiskey over two ice cubes and stirred it with his finger.

He turned on the television and found an old movie starring Wallace Beery and Marie Dressler. He'd seen it at least half a dozen times, but he kept it on just the same. The repetition, the dependable order of the sequential scenes – through thousands of showings in movie theaters and on television – gave him a sense of stability and soothed his nerves. He watched Wallace Beery's clumsy romantic pass at Marie Dressler, and the familiarity of Beery's antics, seen so often before and in that same exact detail, was like a balm on his troubled mind.

At 11:05 the telephone rang.

He finally answered it, declined to do a press interview, and hung up.

At 11:26 it rang again.

This time it was the insurance agent with whom the Merchants' Association had taken out a year's policy on the Mustang. He wanted to know if the coverage was adequate or whether Chase would like to increase it for a nominal sum. He was chatty at first but less so when Chase said that the coverage was adequate.

At 11:50 the phone rang a third time. When Chase answered, the killer said, 'Hello, how has

your morning been?' His voice was hoarse, hardly
louder than a whisper.

'Not good.'

'Did you see the papers?'

'One.'

'Lovely coverage.'

Chase said nothing.

The man said, 'Most people want fame.'

'Not me.'

'Some people would kill for it.'

'You?'

'I'm not after fame,' said the killer.

'What are you after?'

'Meaning, purpose.'

'There is none.'

The killer was silent. Then: 'You're a strange
egg, Mr. Chase.'

Chase relied on silence.

'Be by your phone at six o'clock this evening,
Mr. Chase. It's important.'

'I'm tired of this.'

'*You're* tired? *I'm* doing all the work here. I've
spent the morning researching your background,
and I have similar plans for the afternoon. At
six I'll tell you what I've found.'

Chase said, 'Why?'

'I can't very well pass judgment on you until I
know what sort of transgressions you're guilty of,
can I?' Under the pervading wheeze of protesting

vocal cords lay a trace of the amusement that Chase had previously noticed. 'You see, I didn't randomly select which fornicators I would punish up on Kanackaway.'

'You didn't?'

'No, I researched the situation. I went up there every night for two weeks and copied license-plate numbers. Then I matched them until I found the one most often repeated.'

'Why?'

'To discover the most deserving sinners,' the stranger said. 'In this state, for two dollars, the Bureau of Motor Vehicles will trace a license number for you. I had that done and learned the identity of the boy who owned the car. From there it was a simple matter to investigate his background and to learn the name of his partner in these activities.' The formality of his speech led him into odd locutions – or evasions. 'She wasn't the only young woman he entertained on Kanackaway, even though she thought he was seeing no one else. She had her own promiscuous affairs too. I followed her twice when other boys picked her up, and one of those times she gave herself to the date.'

'Why don't you just stay home and watch old movies?' Chase wondered.

'What?'

'Or seek counseling.'

'I'm not in need of counseling. This sick *world* is in need of counseling. The *world*, not me.' His anger sent him into another coughing fit. Then: 'They were both sluts, the boy as well as the girl. They deserved what they got – except she didn't get hers, thanks to you.'

Chase waited.

The man said, 'You see, I must research you as thoroughly as I did these two. Otherwise, I would never be sure if you deserved the judgment of death or whether I'd eliminated you simply because you'd interfered with my plans and I wanted revenge. In short, I'm not killing people. I'm executing those who deserve it.'

Chase said, 'I don't want you calling here again.'

'Yes, you do.'

Chase didn't reply.

'I'm your motivation,' said the killer.

'My motivation?'

'There's a destiny here.'

'My motivation to do what?'

'That,' said the killer, 'is for you to decide.'

'I'll have the line bugged.'

'That won't stop me,' the stranger said, again amused. 'I'll simply place the phone calls from various booths around the city, and I'll keep them too short to trace.'

'If I refuse to answer my phone?'

'You'll answer it. Six o'clock this evening,' he reminded Chase, and he hung up.

Chase dropped the receiver, uneasily aware that the killer knew him better than he knew himself. He would answer every time, of course. And for the same reasons that he had answered all the nuisance calls of the last few weeks rather than obtain an unlisted number. The only problem was that he didn't know just what those reasons were.

Impulsively, he lifted the receiver and placed a call to the police headquarters downtown. It was the first time in ten and a half months that he had initiated a call.

When the desk sergeant answered, Chase asked for Detective Wallace.

Wallace came on the line a moment later. 'Yes, Mr. Chase, can I help you?'

Chase didn't mention the calls from the killer – which had been why he thought he'd phoned Wallace. Instead he asked, 'How's the investigation coming along?'

Wallace was not averse to talking shop. 'Slowly but surely. We found prints on the knife. If he's ever been arrested for a serious crime or worked for any branch of government, we'll have him soon.'

'And if he's never been printed?'

Wallace said, 'We'll get him anyway. We found a man's ring in the Chevy. It didn't belong to the dead boy, and it looks as if it would be too small for your fingers by a size or three. Didn't lose a ring, did you?'

'No,' Chase said.

'I thought so. Should have called you on it, but I was pretty sure about it. It's his, right enough.'

'Anything else besides the prints and ring?'

'We're keeping a constant watch on the girl and her parents, though I'd appreciate it if you didn't say anything about that to anyone.'

'You think he might try for her?'

'Maybe. If he thinks she can identify him. You know, it's occurred to me that we wouldn't be far off if we gave you a tail as well. Have you thought of that?'

Alarmed out of proportion by the suggestion, Chase said, 'No. I don't see what value that would have.'

'Well, the story was in the papers this morning. He probably doesn't fear you identifying him as much as he does the girl, but he might bear a grudge against you.'

'Grudge? He'd have to be nuts.'

Wallace laughed. 'Well, if not nuts, what *is* he?'

'You mean you've found no motives from questioning the girl, no old lovers who might have –'

'No,' Wallace said. 'Right now we're operating on the assumption there's no rational motive, that he's psychotic.'

'I see.'

'Well,' Wallace said, 'I'm sorry there isn't more solid news.'

'And I'm sorry to have bothered you,' Chase said.

He hung up without telling Wallace about the calls that he had received from the killer, though he had intended to spill it all. A twenty-four-hour guard on the girl. They would do the same to him, if they knew that he'd been contacted.

The walls seemed to sway, alternately closing in like the jaws of an immense vise and swinging away from him as if they were flat gray gates. The floor rose and fell – or seemed to.

A sense of extreme instability overcame him, a sense that the world was not a solid place but as fluid as a shimmering mirage: the very thing that had landed him in the hospital and had eventually led to his seventy-five-percent disability pension. He could not let it grip him again, and he knew that the best way to fight it was to constrict the perimeters of his world, take solace from solitude. He got another drink.

The telephone woke him from his nap just as the dead men touched him with soft, white, corrupted hands.

He sat straight up in bed and cried out, his arms held before him to ward off their cold touch.

When he saw where he was and that he was alone, he sank back, exhausted, and listened to the phone. After thirty rings, he had no choice but to pick it up.

'Yes.'

'I was about to come check on you,' Mrs. Fielding said. 'Are you all right?'

'I'm okay.'

'It took you so long to answer.'

'I was asleep.'

She hesitated, as if framing what she was about to say. 'I'm having Swiss steak, mushrooms, baked corn, and mashed potatoes for supper. Would you like to come down? There's more than I can use.'

'I don't think – '

'A strapping boy like you needs his regular meals.'

'I've already eaten.'

She was silent. Then she said, 'All right. But I wish you'd waited, 'cause I got all this food.'

'I'm sorry, but I'm stuffed,' he said.

'Tomorrow night, maybe.'

'Maybe,' he said. He rang off before she could suggest a late-night snack together.

The ice had melted in his glass, diluting what whiskey he had not drunk. He emptied the watered booze into the bathroom sink, got new ice and a new shot of liquor. It tasted as sour as a bite of lemon rind. He drank it anyway. The cupboard and refrigerator contained nothing else but a bag of Winesap apples.

He turned on the small black-and-white television again and slowly cycled through all the local channels. Nothing but news, news, news, and a cartoon program. He watched the cartoons.

None was amusing.

After the cartoons, he watched an old movie.

Except for the telephone call he'd been told to expect at six o'clock, he had the whole evening ahead of him.

At six o'clock on the nose, the phone rang.

'Hello?'

'Good evening, Chase,' the killer said. His voice was still rough.

Chase sat on the bed.

'How are you tonight?' the killer asked.

'Okay.'

'You know what I've been up to all day?'

'Research.'

'That's right.'

'Tell me what you found,' Chase said, as if it would be news to him even though he was the subject. And maybe it *would* be.

'First, you were born here a little over twenty-four years ago on June 11, 1947, in Mercy Hospital. Your parents died in an auto accident a couple of years ago. You went to school at State and graduated in a three-year accelerated program, having majored in business administration. You did well in all subjects except a few required courses, chiefly Basic Physical Sciences, Biology I and II, Chemistry I and Basic Composition.' The killer whispered on for two or three minutes, reciting biographical facts that Chase had thought private. Courthouse records, college files, newspaper morgues, and half a dozen other sources had provided the killer with far more information about Chase's life than could have been gleaned merely from the recent articles in the *Press-Dispatch*.

'I think I've been on the line too long,' the killer said. 'It's time I went to another booth. Is your phone tapped, Chase?'

'No.'

'Just the same, I'll hang up now and call you back in a few minutes.' The line went dead.

Five minutes later the killer called again.

'What I gave you before was just so much dry grass, Chase. But let me add a few more things and do some speculating. Let's see if I can add a match to it.'

'Whatever you have to do.'

'For one thing,' the man said, 'you inherited a lot of money, but you haven't spent much of it.'

'Not a lot.'

'Forty thousand after taxes, but you live frugally.'

'How would you know that?'

'I drove by your house today and discovered that you live in a furnished apartment on the third floor. When I saw you coming home, it was apparent that you don't spend much on clothes. Until that pretty new Mustang, you didn't have a car. It follows, then, that you must have a great deal of your inheritance left, what with the monthly disability pension from the government to pay most or all of your bills.'

'I want you to stop checking on me.'

The man laughed. 'Can't stop. Remember the necessity to evaluate your moral content before passing judgment, Mr. Chase.'

Chase hung up this time. Having taken the initiative cheered him a little. When the phone began to ring again, he summoned the will not to answer it. After thirty rings, it stopped.

When the ringing began again, ten minutes later, he finally picked it up and said hello.

The killer was furious, straining his damaged throat to the limit. 'If you ever do that to me again, then I'll make sure it isn't a quick, clean kill. I'll see to that. You understand me?'

Chase was silent.

'Mr. Chase?' A beat. 'What's *wrong* with you?'

'Wish I knew,' Chase said.

The stranger decided to let his anger go, and he fell into his previous tone of forced irony:

'That "wounded in action" bit excites me, Mr. Chase. That part of your biography. Because you don't appear disabled enough to deserve a pension, and you more than held your own in our fight. That gives me ideas, makes me think your most serious wounds aren't physical at all.'

'Whose are?'

'I think you had psychological problems that put you in that army hospital and got you a discharge.'

Chase said nothing.

'And you tell *me* that I need counseling. I'll have to take more time to check into this. Very interesting. Well, rest easy tonight, Mr. Chase. You're not scheduled to die yet.'

'Wait.'

'Yes?'

'I have to have a name for you. I can't go on thinking of you in totally impersonal terms like "the man" and "the stranger" and "the killer." Do you see how that is?'

'Yes,' the man admitted.

'A name?'

He considered. Then he said, 'You can call me Judge.'

'Judge?'

'Yes, as in "judge, jury, and executioner." ' He laughed until he coughed, and then he hung up as if he were just an anonymous prankster who had phoned to ask if Chase had Prince Albert in a can.

Chase went to the refrigerator and got an apple. He peeled it and cut it into eight sections, chewing each thoroughly. It wasn't much of a dinner. But there were a lot of energy-giving calories in a glass of whiskey, so he poured a few ounces over ice, for dessert.

He washed his hands, which had become sticky with apple juice.

He would have washed them even if they hadn't been sticky. He washed his hands frequently. Ever since Nam. Sometimes he washed them so often in a single day that they became red and chapped.

With another drink, he went to the bed and watched a movie on TV. He tried not to think about anything except the satisfying daily routines to which he was accustomed: breakfast at Woolworth's, paperback novels, old movies on television, the forty thousand of go-to-hell money in his savings account, his pension check, and the good folks in Tennessee who made Jack Daniel's. Those were the things that counted, that made his small world satisfying and safe.

Again, he refrained from calling the police.

4

The nightmares were so bad that Chase slept fitfully, waking repeatedly at the penultimate moment of horror, as he was surrounded by the tight circle of dead men, as their silent accusations began, as they closed in on him with their hands outstretched.

He rose early, abandoning any hope of rest. He bathed, shaved, and washed his hands with special attention to the dirt under his fingernails.

He sat at the table and peeled an apple for breakfast. He did not want to face the regular customers at Woolworth's lunch counter now that he was more than just another face to them, yet he couldn't think of any place where he might go unrecognized.

It was 9:35, much too early to begin drinking. He observed few rules, but never drinking before lunch was one of them. He seldom broke that one. Afternoons and evenings were for drinking.

Mornings were for remorse, regret, and silent repentance.

But what could he do with the long hours until noon? Filling time without drinking was increasingly difficult.

He turned on the television but couldn't find any old movies. Turned it off.

At last, with nothing to do, he began to recall the details of the nightmare that had awakened him, and that was no good. That was dangerous.

He picked up the phone and placed another call.

It rang three times before a pert young woman answered. She said, 'Dr. Fauvel's office, Miss Pringle speaking, can I help you?'

Chase said, 'I'd like to see the doctor.'

'Are you a regular patient?'

'Yes. My name's Ben Chase.'

'Oh, yes!' Miss Pringle gasped, as though it was a small joy to be hearing from him. 'Good morning, Mr. Chase.' She rattled the pages of an appointment book. 'Your regularly scheduled visit is this Friday afternoon at three.'

'I have to see Dr. Fauvel before that.'

'Tomorrow morning we have half an hour –'

Chase interrupted her. 'Today.'

'I beg your pardon?' Miss Pringle's pleasure at hearing his voice seemed to have diminished appreciably.

'I want an appointment today,' Chase repeated.

Miss Pringle informed him of the heavy work-load that the doctor carried and of the numerous extra hours in each day that the doctor required to study case histories of new patients.

'Please call Dr. Fauvel himself,' Chase said, 'and see if he can find time for me.'

'Dr. Fauvel is in the middle of an appointment –'

'I'll hold.'

'But it's impossible to –'

'I'll wait.'

With a sigh of exasperation, she put him on hold. A minute later, chagrined, Miss Pringle returned to the phone to tell Chase that he had an appointment at four o'clock this afternoon. Clearly, she was perturbed that the rules should be broken for him. She must have known that the government paid the tab and that Fauvel received less compensation than he would have received from one of the wealthy neurotics on his patient list.

If one had to be psychologically disturbed, it helped to have a *unique* disturbance that intrigued the doctor – and a measure of fame or infamy to ensure special treatment.

* * *

At eleven-thirty, while Chase was dressing to go out for lunch, Judge called again. His voice sounded better, although still far from normal. 'How are you feeling this morning, Mr. Chase?'

Chase waited.

'Be expecting a call at six this evening,' Judge said.

'From whom?'

'Very funny. At six o'clock sharp, Mr. Chase.' Judge spoke with the smooth authority of a man accustomed to being obeyed. 'I will have several interesting points to discuss with you, I'm sure. Have a good day now.'

* * *

The inner office of Fauvel's suite on the eighth floor of the Kaine Building, in the center of the city, did not resemble the standard psychiatrist's therapy room as portrayed in countless films and books. For one thing, it was not small and intimate, not at all reminiscent of the womb. It was a pleasantly large space, perhaps thirty feet by thirty-five, with a high shadow-shrouded ceiling. Two walls held bookshelves floor to ceiling; one wall was dressed with paintings of tranquil country scenes, and the fourth was all windows. The bookshelves contained a handful of expensively bound volumes – and perhaps three hundred glass dogs, none larger than the palm of a man's hand and most a good deal smaller.

Collecting glass dogs was Dr. Fauvel's hobby.

Just as the decor of the room – battered desk, heavily padded armchairs, foot-scarred coffee table – didn't match its function, Dr. Fauvel was unlike any stereotypical image of a psychiatrist, whether by intent or by nature. He was a small but solidly built man, athletic looking, with hair that spilled over his collar in a manner that suggested carelessness rather than style. He always always wore a blue suit cut too long in the trousers and in need of a hot iron.

'Sit down, Ben,' Fauvel said. 'Like something to drink – coffee, tea, a Coke?'

'No, thank you,' Chase said.

No couch was provided. The doctor did not believe in pampering his patients. Chase sat in an armchair.

Fauvel settled into the chair to Chase's right and propped his feet on the coffee table. He urged Chase to follow suit. When they were in a pose of relaxation, he said, 'No preliminaries, then?'

'Not today,' Chase said.

'You're tense, Ben.'

'Yes.'

'Something's happened.'

'Yes.'

'But that's life. Something always happens. We don't live in stasis, frozen in amber.'

'This is more than the usual something,' Chase said.

'Tell me about it.'

Chase was silent.

'You came here to tell me, didn't you?' Fauvel urged.

'Yeah. But . . . talking about a problem sometimes makes it worse.'

'That's never true.'

'Maybe not for you.'

'Not for anyone.'

'To talk about it, I have to think about it, and thinking about it makes me nervous. I like things calm. Still and calm.'

'Want to play some word association?'

Chase hesitated, then nodded, dreading the game that they often used to loosen his tongue. He frequently exposed more of himself in his answers than he wished to reveal. And Fauvel did not play the game according to established rules, but with a swift and vicious directness that cut to the heart of the matter. Nevertheless, Chase said, 'Go on.'

Fauvel said, 'Mother.'

'Dead.'

'Father.'

'Dead.'

Fauvel steepled his fingers as if he were a child playing the see-the-church game. 'Love.'

'Woman.'

'Love.'

'Woman,' Chase repeated.

Fauvel did not look at him but stared studiously at the blue glass terrier on the bookshelf nearest him. 'Don't repeat yourself, please.'

Chase apologized, aware that it was expected. The first time that Fauvel had expected an apology in these circumstances, Chase had been surprised. They were therapist and patient, after all, and it seemed odd for the therapist to foster a dependent relationship in which the patient was encouraged to feel guilty for evasive answers. Session by session, however, he was less surprised at anything that Fauvel might suggest.

The doctor again said, 'Love.'

'Woman.'

'Love.'

'Woman.'

'I asked you not to repeat yourself.'

'I'm not a latent homosexual, if that's what you're after.'

Fauvel said, 'But the simple "woman" is an evasion.'

'Everything is an evasion.'

That observation appeared to surprise the doctor, but not enough to jar him out of the stubborn, wearying routine that he had begun. 'Yes, everything is an evasion. But in this case it's an

egregious evasion, because there *is* no woman.
You won't allow one into your life. So, more honesty, if you will. Love.'

Already Chase was perspiring, and he did not
know why.

'Love,' Fauvel insisted.

'Is a many splendored thing.'

'Unacceptable childishness.'

'Sorry.'

'Love.'

Chase finally said, 'Myself.'

'But that's a lie, isn't it?'

'Yes.'

'Because you don't love yourself.'

'No.'

'Very good,' Fauvel said. Now the interchange
of words went faster, one barked close after the
other, as if speed counted in the scoring. Fauvel
said, 'Hate.'

'You.'

'Funny.'

'Thanks.'

'Hate.'

'Self-destructive.'

'Another evasion. Hate.'

'Army.'

'Hate.'

'Vietnam.'

'Hate.'

'Guns.'

'*Hate.*'

'Zacharia,' Chase said, although he had often sworn never to mention that name again or to remember the man attached to it or, indeed, to recall the events that the man had perpetrated.

'Hate,' Fauvel persisted.

'Another word, please.'

'No. Hate.'

'Lieutenant Zacharia.'

'It goes deeper than Zacharia.'

'I know.'

'Hate.'

'Me,' Chase said.

'And that's the truth, isn't it?'

'Yes.'

After a silence, the doctor said, 'Okay, let's back up from you to Zacharia. Do you remember what Lieutenant Zacharia ordered you to do, Benjamin?'

'Yes, sir.'

'What were those orders?'

'We'd sealed off two back entrances to a Cong tunnel system.'

'And?'

'Lieutenant Zacharia ordered me to clear the last entrance.'

'How did you accomplish that?'

'With a grenade, sir.'

'And?'

'And then before the air around the tunnel face could clear, I went forward.'

'And?'

'And used a machine gun.'

'Good.'

'Not so good, sir.'

'Good that you can at least talk about it.'

Chase was silent.

'What happened then, Benjamin?'

'Then we went down, sir.'

'We?'

'Lieutenant Zacharia, Sergeant Coombs, Privates Halsey and Wade, a couple of other men.'

'And you.'

'Yeah. Me.'

'Then?'

'In the tunnel, we found four dead men and parts of men lying in the foyer of the complex. Lieutenant Zacharia ordered a cautious advance. A hundred fifty yards along, we came to a bamboo gate.'

'Blocking the way.'

'Yeah. Villagers behind it.'

'Tell me about the villagers.'

'Mostly women.'

'How many women, Ben?'

'Maybe twenty.'

'Children?' Fauvel asked.

Silence was a refuge.

'Were there children?'

Chase sank down in the heavy padding of the armchair, shoulders drawn up as if he wished to hide between them. 'A few.'

'They were imprisoned there?'

'No. The bamboo was an obstacle. The Cong tunnels ran a lot deeper than that, a lot farther. We hadn't even reached the weapons cache. The villagers were assisting the Vietcong, collaborating with them, obstructing us.'

'Do you think they were forced to obstruct you, forced by the Vietcong ... or were they willing agents of the enemy?'

Chase was silent.

'I'm waiting for an answer,' Fauvel said sternly.

Chase didn't reply.

'*You* are waiting for an answer,' Fauvel told him, 'whether you realize it or not. Were these villagers being forced to obstruct your advance, forced at gunpoint by the Cong in the tunnels behind them, or were they there at their own choice?'

'Hard to say.'

'Is it?'

'Hard for me, anyway.'

'In those situations you could never be sure.'

'Right.'

'They might have been collaborationists – or they might have been innocent.'

'Right.'

'Okay. Then what happened?'

'We tried to open the gate, but the women were holding it shut with a system of ropes.'

'Women.'

'They used women as a shield. Or sometimes the women were the worst killers of all, cut you down with a smile.'

'So you ordered them out of the way?' Fauvel asked.

'They wouldn't move. The lieutenant said it might be a trap designed to contain us at that point, delay us long enough for the Cong to somehow get behind us.'

'Could that have been true?'

'Could have been.'

'Likely?'

'Yes.'

'Go on.'

'It was dark. There was a smell in that tunnel I can't explain, made up of sweat and urine and rotting vegetables, as heavy as if it had substance. Lieutenant Zacharia ordered us to open fire and clear the way.'

'Did you comply?'

Chase was silent.'

'Did you comply?'

'Not immediately.'

'But eventually?'

'The stench . . . the darkness . . .'

'You complied.'

'So claustrophobic down there, Cong probably coming around behind us through a secret tunnel.'

'So you complied with the order?'

'Yes.'

'You personally – or the squad?'

'The squad and me. Everyone did.'

'You shot them.'

'Cleared the way.'

'Shot them.'

'We could have died there.'

'Shot them.'

'Yeah.'

Fauvel gave him a rest. Half a minute. Then: 'Later, when the tunnel had been cleared, searched, the weapons cache destroyed, then you ran into the ambush that earned you the Medal of Honor.'

'Yes. That was above ground.'

Fauvel said, 'You crawled across the field of fire for nearly two hundred yards and brought back a wounded sergeant named Coombs.'

'Samuel Coombs.'

'You received two minor put painful wounds in the thigh and calf of your right leg, but you didn't stop crawling until you had reached shelter. Then you secured Coombs behind a stand of scrub, and having reached a point on the enemy's flank by means of your heroic crossing of the open field – what happened?'

'I killed some of the bastards.'

'Enemy soldiers.'

'Yeah.'

'How many?'

'Eighteen.'

'Eighteen Vietcong soldiers?'

'Yeah.'

'So you not only saved Sergeant Coombs's life but contributed substantially to the well-being of your entire unit.' He had only slightly paraphrased the wording on the scroll that Chase had received in the mail from the president himself.

Chase said nothing.

'You see where this heroism came from, Ben?'

'We've talked about it before.'

'So you know the answer.'

'It came from guilt.'

'That's right.'

'Because I wanted to die. Subconsciously wanted to be killed, so I rushed onto the field of fire, hoping to be shot down.'

'Do you believe that analysis, or do you think maybe it's just something I made up to degrade your medal?'

Chase said, 'I believe it. I never wanted the medal in the first place.'

'Now,' Fauvel said, unsteepling his fingers, 'let's extend that analysis just a bit. Though you hoped to be shot and killed in that ambush, although you took absurd risks to ensure your death, you lived. And became a national hero.'

'Life's funny, huh?'

'When you learned Lieutenant Zacharia had submitted your name for consideration for the Medal of Honor, you suffered a nervous breakdown that hospitalized you and eventually led to your honorable discharge.'

'I was just burnt out.'

'No, the breakdown was an attempt to punish yourself, once you'd failed to get yourself killed. Punish yourself and escape from your guilt. But the breakdown failed too, because you pulled out of it. Well regarded, honorably discharged, much too strong not to recover psychologically, you still had to carry your burden of guilt.'

Chase was silent again.

Fauvel continued: 'Perhaps when you chanced upon that scene in the park on Kanackaway, you recognized another opportunity to punish yourself. You must have realized that there was a strong possibility you'd be hurt or killed, and you must have subconsciously anticipated your death agreeably enough.'

'You're wrong,' Chase said.

Fauvel was silent.

'You're wrong,' Chase repeated.

'Probably not,' Fauvel said with a hint of impatience, and he used a direct stare to try to make Chase uncomfortable.

'It wasn't like that at all. I had thirty pounds on him, and I knew what I was doing. He was an amateur. He had no hope of really hurting me.'

Fauvel said nothing.

Finally Chase said, 'Sorry.'

Fauvel smiled. 'Well, you aren't a psychiatrist, so we can't expect you to see into it so clearly. You aren't detached from it like I am.' He cleared his throat, looked back at the blue terrier. 'Now that we've come this far – why did you solicit this extra session, Ben?'

Once he began, Chase found the telling easy. In ten minutes he had related the events of the previous day and repeated, almost word for word, the conversations that he'd had with Judge.

When Chase finished, Fauvel asked, 'So. What do you want from me, then?'

'I want to know how to handle it, some advice.'

'I don't advise. I guide and interpret.'

'Some guidance then. When Judge calls, it's more than just the threats that upset me. It's – this feeling I have of being detached, separated from everything.'

'Another breakdown?'

'I feel the edge,' Chase said.

Fauvel said, 'Ignore him.'

'Judge?'

'Ignore him.'

'But don't I have a responsibility to –'

'Ignore him.'

'I can't.'

'You must,' Fauvel said.

'What if he's serious?'

'He's not.'

'What if he's really going to kill me?'

'He won't.'

'How can you be sure?' Chase was perspiring heavily. Great dark circles stained the underarms of his shirt and plastered the cotton to his back.

Fauvel smiled at the blue terrier and shifted his gaze to a glass greyhound blown in amber. The smug, self-assured look was back. 'I can be so sure of that, because Judge does not exist.'

Chase did not immediately understand the reply. When he grasped the import of it, he didn't like it. 'You're saying what – that this Judge isn't real?'

'Is that what you're saying, Chase?'

'No.'

'You're the one who said it.'

'I didn't hallucinate him. None of this. The

part about the murder and the girl are in the papers.'

'Oh, that was real enough,' Fauvel said. 'But these phone calls . . . I don't know. What do you think, Chase?'

Chase was silent.

'Were they real phone calls?'

'Yes.'

'Or imagination?'

'No.'

'Delusions of –'

'No.'

Fauvel said, 'I've noticed for some time that you have begun to shake off this unnatural desire for privacy and that you're gradually facing the world more squarely, week by week.'

'I haven't noticed that.'

'Oh, yes. Subtly, perhaps, but you've grown curious about the rest of the world. You're beginning to be restless about getting on with life.'

Chase didn't feel restless.

He felt cornered.

'Perhaps you're even beginning to experience a reawakening of your sex drive, though not much yet. Guilt overwhelmed you, because you hadn't been punished for the things that happened in that tunnel, and you didn't want to lead a normal life until you felt that you'd suffered enough.'

Chase disliked the doctor's smug self-assurance. Right now all he wanted was to get out of there, to get home and close the door and open the bottle.

Fauvel said, 'You couldn't accept the fact that you wanted to taste the good things of life again, and you invented Judge because he represented the remaining possibility of punishment. You had to make some excuses for being forced into life again, and Judge worked well in this respect too. You would, sooner or later, have to take the initiative to stop him. You could pretend that you still wanted seclusion in which to mourn but were no longer being permitted that indulgence.'

'All wrong,' Chase said. 'Judge is real.'

'Oh, I think not.' Fauvel smiled at the amber greyhound. 'If you really and truly thought this man was real, that these calls to you were real – then why wouldn't you go to the police rather than to your psychiatrist?'

Chase had no answer. 'You're twisting things.'

'No. Just showing you the straight truth.'

'He's real.'

Fauvel stood and stretched. 'I recommend you go home and forget Judge. You don't need an excuse to live like a normal human being. You *have* suffered enough, Ben, more than enough. You made a terrible mistake. All right. But in that tunnel, you were in an incredibly stressful situation, under unendurable pressures. It was a *mistake*, not a calculated savagery. For the lives you took, you saved others. Remember that.'

Chase stood, bewildered, no longer perfectly sure that he did know what was real and what was not.

Fauvel put his arm around Chase's shoulders and walked him to the door. 'Friday at three,' the doctor said. 'Let's see how far out of your hole you've come by then. I think you're going to make it, Ben. Don't despair.'

Miss Pringle escorted him to the outer door of the waiting room and closed it after him, leaving him alone in the hallway.

'Judge is real,' Chase said to no one at all. 'Isn't he?'

5

At six o'clock, Chase was sitting on the edge of his bed by the nightstand and telephone, sipping Jack Daniel's. He put the drink down, wiped his sweaty hands on his slacks, cleared his throat so his voice wouldn't catch when he tried to speak.

At 6:05 he began to feel uneasy. He thought of going downstairs to ask Mrs. Fielding what time her clocks showed, in the event that his own was not functioning properly. He refrained from doing so only because he was afraid of missing the call while downstairs.

At 6:15 he washed his hands.

At 6:30 he went to the cupboard, took down his whiskey bottle of the day – which he'd barely touched – and poured a glassful. He did not put it away again. He read the label, which he had studied a hundred times before, then carried his drink back to the bed.

By seven o'clock he was feeling the liquor. He

settled back against the headboard and finally considered what Fauvel had said: that there was no Judge, that he had been illusory, a psychological mechanism for rationalizing the gradual diminishment of Chase's guilt complex. He tried to think about that, to study the meaning of it, but he could not be sure if this was a good or a bad development.

In the bathroom, he drew a tub of warm water and tested it until it was just right. He folded a damp washcloth on the wide porcelain rim of the tub and placed his drink on that. The whiskey, the water, and the rising steam conspired to make him feel as though he were floating up into soft clouds. He leaned back until his head touched the wall, closed his eyes, and tried not to think about anything – especially blocking all thoughts of Judge and the Medal of Honor and the nine months that he had spent on active duty in Nam.

Unfortunately, he began to think of Louise Allenby, the girl whose life he had saved, and in his mind's eye he saw her small, trembling, bare breasts, which had looked so inviting in the weak light of the car in lovers' lane. The thought, though pleasant enough, was unfortunate because it contributed to his first erection in nearly a year. That development was perhaps desirable; he wasn't sure. But it seemed inappropriate, given the hideous circumstances in which he'd seen the girl half undressed. He was reminded of the blood in the car – and the blood reminded him of the reasons for his recent inability to function as a man. Those reasons were still so formidable that he couldn't face them alone. The erection was short-lived, and when it was gone, he wasn't certain if it indicated an eventual end to his psychological impotency or whether it had resulted only from the warm water.

He got out of the water when his whiskey glass was empty. He was toweling himself when the telephone rang.

The electric clock showed 8:02.

Naked, he sat on the bed and answered the phone.

'Sorry I'm late,' Judge said.

Dr. Fauvel had been wrong.

'I thought you weren't going to call,' Chase said.

'I required a little more time than I'd expected to locate some information on you.'

'What information?'

Judge ignored the question, intent on proceeding in his own fashion. 'So you see a psychiatrist once a week, do you?'

Chase did not reply.

'That alone is fairly good proof that the

accusation I made yesterday is true – that your
disability pension is for mental, not physical,
injuries.'

Chase wished that he had a drink with him,
but he could not ask Judge to hold on while he
poured one. For reasons that he could not
explain, he didn't want Judge to know that he
drank heavily.

Chase said, 'How did you find out?'

'Followed you this afternoon,' Judge said.

'Bold.'

'The righteous can afford to be bold.'

'Of course.'

Judge laughed as if delighted with himself. 'I
saw you going into the Kaine Building, and I got
into the lobby fast enough to see which elevator
you took and which floor you got off at. On the
eighth floor, besides Dr. Fauvel's offices, there are
two dentists and three insurance companies. It
was simple enough to look in the waiting rooms
of those other places and inquire after you, like
a friend, with the secretaries and receptionists.
I left the shrink's place for last, because I just
knew that's where you were. When no one knew
you in the other offices, I didn't have to risk
glancing in Fauvel's waiting room. I knew.'

Chase said, 'So what?'

He hoped that he sounded more nonchalant
than he felt, for it was somehow important to

make the right impression on Judge. He was sweating again. He would need to take another bath by the time this conversation was concluded. And he would need a drink, a cold drink.

'As soon as I knew you were in the psychiatrist's office,' Judge said, 'I decided I had to obtain copies of his personal files on you. I remained in the building, out of sight in a maintenance closet, until all the offices were closed and the employees went home.'

'I don't believe you,' Chase said, aware of what was coming, dreading to hear it.

'You don't *want* to believe me, but you do.' Judge took a long, slow breath before he continued: 'The eighth floor was clear by six o'clock. By six-thirty I got the door open to Dr. Fauvel's suite. I know a little about such things, and I was very careful. I didn't damage the lock, and I didn't trip any alarms because there was none. I required an additional half an hour to locate his files and to secure your records, which I copied on his photocopier.'

'Breaking and entering – then theft,' Chase said.

'But it hardly matters on top of murder, does it?'

'You admit that what you've done is murder.'

'No. Judgment. But the authorities don't understand. They call it murder. They're part of the problem. They're not good facilitators.'

Chase said nothing.

'You'll receive in the mail, probably the day after tomorrow, complete copies of Dr. Fauvel's notes on you, along with copies of several articles he's written for various medical journals. You're mentioned in all these and are, in some of them, the sole subject of discussion. Not by name. "Patient C," he calls you. But it's clearly you.'

Chase said, 'I didn't know he'd done that.'

'They're interesting articles, Chase. They'll give you some idea of what he thinks of you.' Judge's tone changed, became more contemptuous. 'Reading those records, Chase, I found more than enough to permit me to pass judgment on you.'

'Oh?'

'I read all about how you got your Medal of Honor.'

Chase waited.

'And I read about the tunnels and what you did in them – and how you failed to expose Lieutenant Zacharia when he destroyed the evidence and falsified the report. Do you think the Congress would have voted you the Medal of Honor if they knew you killed civilians, Chase?'

'Stop.'

'You killed women, didn't you?'

'Maybe.'

'You killed women and children, Chase, non-combatants.'

'I'm not sure if I killed anyone,' Chase said more to himself than to Judge. 'I pulled the trigger . . . but I was . . . firing wildly at the walls . . . I don't know.'

'Noncombatants.'

'You don't know what it was like.'

'Children, Chase.'

'You know nothing about me.'

'You killed children. What kind of animal are you, Chase?'

'Fuck you!' Chase had come to his feet as if something had exploded close behind him. 'What would you know about it? Were you ever over there, did you ever have to serve in that stinking country?'

'Some patriotic paean to duty won't change my mind, Chase. We all love this country, but most of us realize there are limits to – '

'Bullshit,' Chase said.

He could not remember having been this angry in all the time since his breakdown. Now and then he had been irritated by something or someone, but he had never allowed himself to feel extremes of emotion.

'Chase – '

'I bet you were all for the war. I'll bet you're one of the people that made it possible for me to be there in the first place. It's easy to set standards of performance, select limits of right and wrong, when you never get closer than ten thousand miles to the place where it's all coming down.'

Judge tried to speak, but Chase talked him down:

'I didn't even *want* to be there. I didn't believe in it, and I was scared shitless the whole time. All I thought about was staying alive. In that tunnel, I couldn't think of anything else. I wasn't *me*. I was a textbook case of paranoia, living in blind terror, just trying to get through.'

He had never spoken about the experience so directly or at such length to anyone, not even to Fauvel, who had pried his story from him in single words and sentence fragments.

'You're eaten with guilt,' Judge said.

'That doesn't matter.'

'I think it does. It proves you know you did wrong and you – '

'It *doesn't* matter, because regardless of how guilty I feel, you haven't the right to pass judgment on me. You're sitting there with your little list of commandments, but you've never been anywhere that made a list seem pointless, anywhere that circumstances forced you to act in a way you loathed.'

Chase was amazed to realize that he was

crying. He had not cried in a long time.

'You're rationalizing,' Judge began, trying to regain control of the conversation. 'You're a despicable, murdering –'

Chase said, 'You've not exactly followed that commandment yourself. You killed Michael Karnes.'

'There was a difference,' Judge said. Some of the hoarseness had returned to his voice.

'Oh?'

'Yes,' Judge said defensively. 'I studied his situation carefully, collected evidence against him, and only then passed judgment. You didn't do any of that, Chase. You killed perfect strangers, and you very likely murdered innocents who had no black marks on their souls.'

Chase hung up.

When the phone rang at four different times during the following hour, he was able to ignore it completely. His anger remained sharp, the strongest emotion that he had experienced in long months of near catatonia.

He drank three more glasses of whiskey before he began to feel mellow again. The tremors in his hands gradually subsided.

A ten o'clock he dialed the number of police headquarters and asked for Detective Wallace, who at that moment was out.

He tried again at 10:40. This time Wallace was

in and willing to speak to him.

'Nothing's going as well as we hoped,' Wallace said. 'This guy doesn't seem to have been printed. At least, he's not among the most obvious profile group of felons. We still might find him in another group – military files or something.'

'What about the ring?'

'Turns out to be a cheap accessory that sells at under fifteen bucks retail in about every store in the state. Impossible to keep track of where and when and to whom a particular ring might have been sold.'

Chase committed himself reluctantly. 'Then I have something for you,' he said. In a few short sentences, he told the detective abut Judge's calls.

Wallace was angry, though he made an effort not to shout. 'Why in the hell didn't you let us know about this before?'

'I thought, with the prints, you'd be sure to get him.'

'Prints hardly ever make a difference in a situation like this,' Wallace said. There was still a bite in his voice, though it was softer now. He had evidently remembered that his informant was a war hero.

'Besides,' Chase said, 'the killer realized the chance of the line being tapped. He's been calling from pay phones and keeping the calls under five minutes.'

'Just the same, I'd like to hear him. I'll be over with a man in fifteen minutes.'

'Just one man?'

Wallace said, 'We'll try not to upset your routine too much.'

Chase almost laughed at that.

* * *

From his third-floor window, Chase watched for the police. He met them at the front door to avoid Mrs. Fielding's involvement.

Wallace introduced the plainclothes officer who came with him: James Tuppinger. Tuppinger was six inches taller than Wallace — and not drab looking. He wore his blond hair in such a short crew cut that he appeared almost bald from a distance. His eyes were blue and moved from one object to another with the swift, penetrating glance of an accountant itemizing an inventory. He carried a large suitcase.

Mrs. Fielding watched from the living room, where she pretended to be engrossed in a television program, but she did not come out to see what was happening. Chase got the two men upstairs before she could learn who they were.

'Cozy little place you have,' Wallace said.

'It's enough for me,' Chase said.

Tuppinger's gaze flicked about, catching the unmade bed, the dirty whiskey glasses on the counter, and the half-empty bottle of liquor. He did not say anything. He took his suitcase full of tools to the phone, put it down, and began examining the lead-in wires that came through the wall near the base of the single window.

While Tuppinger worked, Wallace questioned Chase. 'What did he sound like on the phone?'

'Hard to say.'

'Old? Young?'

'In between.'

'Accent?'

'No.'

'Speech impediment?'

'No. Just hoarse – apparently from the struggle we had.'

Wallace said, 'Can you remember what he said, each time he called?'

'Approximately.'

'Tell me.' He slumped down in the only easy chair in the room and crossed his legs. He looked as if he had fallen asleep, though he was alert.

Chase told Wallace everything that he could remember about the strange conversations with Judge. The detective had a few questions that stirred a few additional details from Chase's memory.

'He sounds like a religious psychotic,' Wallace said. 'All this stuff about fornication and sin and passing judgments.'

'Maybe. But I wouldn't look for him at tent meetings. I think it's more of a moral excuse to kill than a genuine belief.'

'Maybe,' Wallace said. 'Then again, we get his sort every once in a while.'

Jim Tuppinger finished his work. He outlined the workings of his listening and recording equipment and further explained the trace equipment that the telephone company would use to seek Judge when he called.

'Well,' Wallace said, 'tonight, for once, I intend to go home when my shift ends.' Just the thought of eight hours' sleep made his lids droop over his weary, bloodshot eyes.

'One thing,' Chase said.

'Yeah?'

'If this leads to something – do you have to tell the press about my part in it?'

'Why?' Wallace asked.

'It's just that I'm tired of being a celebrity, of having people bother me at all hours of the day and night.'

'It has to come out in the trial, if we nab him,' Wallace said.

'But not before?'

'I guess not.'

'I'd appreciate it,' Chase said. 'In any case, I'll have to appear at the trial, won't I?'

'Probably.'

'If the press didn't have to know until then, it would cut down on the news coverage by half.'

'You really *are* modest, aren't you?' Wallace asked. Before Chase could respond to that, the detective smiled, clapped him on the shoulder, and left.

'Would you like a drink?' Chase asked Tuppinger.

'Not on duty.'

'Mind if I –?'

'No. Go ahead.'

Chase noticed that Tuppinger watched him with interest as he got new ice cubes and poured a large dose of whiskey. It wasn't as large as usual. He supposed he'd have to restrain his thirst with the cop around.

When Chase sat on the bed, Tuppinger said, 'I read all about your exploits over there.'

'Oh?'

'Really something,' Tuppinger said.

'Not really.'

'Oh, yes, really,' Tuppinger insisted. He was sitting in the easy chair, which he had moved close to his equipment. 'It had to be hard over there, worse than anybody at home could ever know.'

Chase nodded.

'I'd imagine the medals don't mean much. I mean, considering everything you had to go through to earn them, they must seem kind of insignificant.'

Chase looked up from his drink, surprised at the insight. 'You're right. They don't mean anything.'

Tuppinger said, 'And it must be hard to come back from a place like that and settle into a normal life. Memories couldn't fade that quickly.'

Chase started to respond, then saw Tuppinger glance meaningfully at the glass of whiskey in his hand. He closed his mouth, bit off his response. Then, hating Tuppinger as badly as he hated Judge, he lifted the drink and took a large swallow.

He said, 'I'll have another, I think. Sure you don't want one?'

'Positive,' Tuppinger said.

When Chase returned to the bed with another glassful, Tuppinger cautioned him against answering the phone without first waiting for the tape to be started. Then he went into the bathroom, where he remained almost ten minutes.

When the cop returned, Chase asked, 'How late do we have to stay up?'

'Has he ever called this late — except that first night?'

'No,' Chase said.

'Then I'll turn in now,' Tuppinger said, flopping in the easy chair. 'See you in the morning.'

* * *

In the morning, the whispers of the dead men woke Chase, but they proved to be nothing more than the sound of water running in the bathroom sink. Having risen first, Tuppinger was shaving.

When the cop opened the door and came into the main room of the tiny efficiency apartment a few minutes later, he looked refreshed. 'All yours!' He seemed remarkably energetic for having spent the night in the armchair.

Chase took his time bathing and shaving, because the longer he remained in the bathroom, the less he would have to talk to the cop. When he was finally finished, it was 9:45. Judge had not yet called.

'What have you got for breakfast?' Tuppinger asked.

'Sorry. There isn't anything here.'

'Oh, you've got to have something. Doesn't have to be breakfast food. I'm not particular in the morning. I'll eat a cheese sandwich as happily as bacon and eggs.'

Chase opened the refrigerator and took out the bag of Winesap apples. 'Only these.'

Tuppinger stared at the apples and into the

empty refrigerator. He glanced at the whiskey bottle on the counter. He didn't say anything.

'They'll do fine,' Tuppinger said enthusiastically, taking the clear plastic bag of apples from Chase. 'Want one?'

'No.'

'You ought to eat breakfast,' Tuppinger said. 'Even something small. Gets the stomach working, sharpens you for the day ahead.'

'No, thanks.'

Tuppinger carefully peeled two apples, sectioned them, and ate them slowly, chewing well.

By 10:30 Chase was worried. Suppose Judge did not call today? The idea of having Tuppinger here for the afternoon and the evening, of waking up again to the sound of Tuppinger in the bathroom shaving, was all but intolerable.

'Do you have a relief man?' Chase asked.

'Unless it gets too protracted,' Tuppinger said, 'I'll stick with it myself.'

'How long might that be?'

'Oh,' Tuppinger said, 'if we don't have it wrapped up in forty-eight hours, I'll call in my relief.'

Though another forty-eight hours with Tuppinger was in no way an attractive prospect, it was probably no worse – perhaps better – than it would have been with another cop. Tuppinger was too observant for comfort, but he didn't talk much. Let him look. And let him think whatever he wanted to think. As long as he could keep his mouth shut, they wouldn't have any problems.

At noon Tuppinger ate two more apples and cajoled Chase into eating most of one. They decided that Chase would go for take-out fried chicken, fries, and slaw at dinnertime.

At 12:30 Chase had his first Jack Daniel's of the day.

Tuppinger watched, but he didn't say anything.

Chase didn't offer him a drink this time.

At three in the afternoon the telephone rang. Although this was what they had been waiting for since the night before, Chase didn't want to answer it. Because Tuppinger was there, urging him to pick it up while he adjusted his own earphones, he finally lifted the receiver.

'Hello?' His voice sounded cracked, strained.

'Mr. Chase?'

'Yes,' he said, immediately recognizing the voice. It was not Judge.

'This is Miss Pringle, calling for Dr. Fauvel, to remind you of your appointment tomorrow at three. You have a fifty-minute session scheduled, as usual.'

'Thank you.' This double check was a strict routine with Miss Pringle, although Chase had forgotten about it.

'Tomorrow at three,' she repeated, then hung up.

* * *

At ten till five, Tuppinger complained of hunger and of a deep reluctance to consume a fifth Winesap apple.

Chase didn't object to an early dinner, accepted Tuppinger's money, and went out to buy the chicken, French fries, and slaw. He purchased a large Coca-Cola for Tuppinger but nothing for himself. He would drink his usual.

They ate at a quarter past five, without dinner conversation, watching an old movie on television.

Less than two hours later Wallace arrived, looking thoroughly weary although he had only come on duty at six. He said, 'Mr. Chase, do you think I might have a word alone with Jim?'

'Sure,' Chase said.

He stepped into the bathroom, closed the door, and turned on the water in the sink, which made a sound like dead men whispering. The noise put him on edge.

He lowered the lid of the commode and sat facing the empty tub, realizing that it needed to be scrubbed. He wondered if Tuppinger had noticed.

Less than five minutes passed before Wallace

knocked on the door. 'Sorry to push you out of your own place like that. Police business.'

'We haven't been lucky, as Mr. Tuppinger probably told you.'

Wallace nodded. He looked peculiarly sheepish, and for the first time he could not meet Chase's gaze. 'I've heard.'

'It's the longest he's gone without calling.'

Wallace nodded. 'It's possible, you know, that he won't be calling at all, any more.'

'You mean, since he passed judgment on me?'

Chase saw that Tuppinger was disconnecting wires and packing his equipment into the suitcase.

Wallace said, 'I'm afraid you're right, Mr. Chase. The killer has passed his judgment – or lost interest in you, one or the other – and he isn't going to try to contact you again. We don't want to keep a man tied up here.'

'You're leaving?' Chase asked.

'Well, yeah, it seems best.'

'But another few hours might – '

'Might produce nothing,' Wallace said. 'What we're going to do, Mr. Chase, is we're going to rely on you to tell us what Judge says if, as seems unlikely now, he should call again.' He smiled at Chase.

In that smile was all the explanation that Chase required. He said, 'When Tuppinger sent me out for dinner, he called you, didn't he?' Not waiting for a response, he went on: 'And he told you about the call from Dr. Fauvel's secretary – the word "session" probably alarmed him. And now you've talked to the good doctor.'

Tuppinger finished packing the equipment. He hefted the case and looked quickly around the room to be sure that he had not left anything behind.

'Judge is real,' Chase told Wallace.

'I'm sure that he is,' Wallace said. 'That's why I want you to report any calls he might make to you.' But his tone was that of an adult humoring a child.

'You stupid bastard, he *is* real!'

Wallace flushed with anger. When he spoke, there was tension in his voice, and his controlled tone was achieved with obvious effort. 'Mr. Chase, you saved the girl. You deserve to be praised for that. But the fact remains, no one has called here in nearly twenty-four hours. And if you believed such a man as Judge existed, you surely would've contacted us before this, when he first called. It would've been natural for you to rush to us – especially a duty-conscious young man like yourself. All these things, examined in the light of your psychiatric record and Dr. Fauvel's explanations, make it clear that the expenditure of one of our best men isn't required.

Tuppinger has other duties.'

Chase saw how overwhelmingly the evidence seemed to point to Fauvel's thesis, just as he saw how his own behaviour hadn't helped him. His fondness for whiskey in front of Tuppinger. His inability to carry on a simple conversation. Worst of all, his anxiety about publicity might have appeared to be the insincere protestations of a man who, in fact, wanted attention. Still, with his fists balled at his sides, he said, 'Get out.'

'Take it easy, son,' Wallace said.

'Get out right now.'

Wallace looked around the room and let his attention come to rest on the bottle of whiskey. 'Tuppinger tells me you haven't any food on hand, but that there are five bottles in that cupboard.' He did not look at Chase. He seemed to be embarrassed by Tuppinger's obvious spying. 'You look thirty pounds underweight, son.'

'Get out,' Chase repeated.

Wallace was not ready to leave yet. He was searching for some way to soften the accusation implicit in their departure. But then he sighed and said, 'Son, no matter what happened to you over there in Vietnam, you aren't going to forget about it with whiskey.'

Before Chase, infuriated at the homespun psychoanalysis, could order him out again, Wallace finally left with Jim Tuppinger at his heels.

Chase closed the door after them. Quietly.
He locked it.
He poured a drink.
He was alone again. But he was accustomed
to being alone.

6

Thursday evening at seven-thirty, having successfully evaded Mrs. Fielding on his way out of the house, Chase drove his Mustang to Kanackaway Ridge Road, aware and yet unaware of his destination. He stayed within the speed limits through Ashside and the outlying districts, but floored the accelerator at the bottom of the mountain road, taking the wide curves on the far outside. The white guard rails slipped past so quickly and so close on the right that they blurred into a continuous wall of pale planking, the cables between them like black scrawls on the phantom boards.

On the top of the ridge, he parked where he had pulled off the road Monday night, killed the engine. He slouched in his seat, listening to the whispering breeze.

He should never have stopped, should have kept moving at all costs. As long as he was moving, he did not have to wonder what to do next. Stopped, he was perplexed, frustrated, restless.

He got out of the car, uncertain of what he expected to find here that would be of any help to him. A good hour of daylight remained in which to search the area where the Chevy had been parked. But, of course, the police would have combed and recombed it far more thoroughly than he ever could.

He strolled along the edge of the park to the bramble row where the Chevy had been. The sod was well trampled, littered with half-smoked cigarette butts, candy wrappers, and balled-up pages from a reporter's notepad. He kicked at the debris and scanned the mashed grass, feeling ridiculous. Too many morbid curiosity seekers had been here. He wouldn't find a clue in all this mess.

Next he went to the railing at the edge of the cliff, leaned against it, and stared down the wall of rock to the tangled patch of brambles and locust trees far below. When he raised his head, he could see the entire city spread along the valley. In the summer evening light, the green copper dome of the courthouse was like a structure out of a fairy tale.

He was still gazing at that corroded curve of metal when he heard a sharp whine. And again.

The steel handrail shivered under his hands. An old war sound: a bullet slapping metal, ricocheting.

With a quickness honed in combat, he dropped to the ground, surveyed the park, and decided that the nearest row of shrubs was the best cover. He rolled toward that hedgerow and came up against the thorns so hard that he tore his cheek and forehead.

He lay motionless. Waiting.

A minute passed. Another. No sound but the wind.

Chase crawled on his stomach to the far end of the bramble row, which paralleled the highway. He eased into the open, looked to his right, and saw that the park appeared to be deserted.

He started to get up and turn toward the highway, then fell back again. Instinct. Where he'd been, the grass flew into the air, torn loose by a bullet. Judge had a pistol fitted with a sound suppressor.

No one in civilian life could have legal access to a silencer. Evidently Judge had black-market resources.

Chase scrambled back along the shrubs, the way he had come, to the middle of the hedgerow. Swiftly he took off his shirt, tore it in two pieces, and wrapped his hands with the cloth. Lying on his stomach, he pressed the thorny vines apart until he opened a chink through which he could survey the land immediately beyond.

He saw Judge at once. The man was huddled by the front fender of Chase's Mustang, down on one knee, the pistol held at arm's length as he waited for his prey to appear. Two hundred feet away, in the weak light of the dusk, he was well shielded from Chase, little more than a dark figure; his face was but a blur in veils of shadow.

Chase let go of the brambles and stripped the cloth from his hands. He had minor nicks on the tips of three fingers, but he was for the most part unscathed.

To his right, no more than four feet away, a bullet snapped through the brambles, spraying chopped leaves. Another passed at the level of Chase's head, no more than two feet to his left, and then another still farther to the left.

Judge did not have the nerves of a professional killer. Tired of waiting, he had begun to fire blindly, wasting ammunition, hoping for a lucky hit.

Chase crawled back toward the right end of the row.

He peered out cautiously and saw Judge leaning against the car, attempting to reload his pistol. His head was bent over the gun, and although it should have been a simple task, he was fumbling nervously with the clip.

Chase went for the bastard.

He had covered only a third of the distance between them when Judge heard him coming. The killer looked up, still a cipher in the waning light, twisted around the end of the car, and sprinted along the highway.

Chase was underweight and out of shape, but he was gaining.

The road crested a rise and sloped so sharply that Chase was forced to put less effort into his pursuit lest he pitch forward and lose his balance.

Ahead, a red Volkswagen was parked along the shoulder of the highway. Judge reached the car, got behind the wheel, and swung the door shut. He had left the engine running. The Volkswagen instantly pulled away. Its tires hit the asphalt, spun briefly, shrieking and kicking up thick smoke; then the car shot down Kanackaway Ridge Road.

Chase didn't have a chance to catch even part of the license-plate number, because he was startled by an air horn frighteningly close behind.

He leaped sideways off the road, tripped, rolled on the gravel verge, hugging himself for protection from the stones.

Brakes barked just once, like the cry of a wounded man. A large moving van – with dark

letters against its orange side: U-HAUL –
boomed past, moving much too fast on the steep
incline of Kanackaway Ridge Road, swaying
slightly as its load shifted.

Then both the car and truck were out of sight.

7

A two-inch scratch on his forehead and a smaller scratch on his cheek, inflicted by the thorns in the bramble row, were already crusted with dried blood. The tips of three fingers also were scarred by the brambles, but with all his other pains, he didn't even feel these minor wounds. His ribs ached from the roll he'd taken on the gravel shoulder of Kanackaway Ridge Road – although none seemed broken when he pressed on them – and his chest, back, and arms were bruised where the largest stones had dug in as he tumbled over them. Both his knees were skinned. He had lost his shirt, of course, when he ripped it in two as protection from the thorns, and his trousers were fit only for the trash can.

He sat in the Mustang by the edge of the park, assessing the damage, and he was so angry that he wanted to strike at something, anything. Instead, he waited, cooled off, settled down.

Already, in the early darkness, a few cars had arrived at lovers' lane, driving over the sod to the hedges. Chase was amazed that all these young lovers were returning unfazed to the scene of the murder, apparently unconcerned that the man who had knifed Michael Karnes was still on the loose. He wondered if they would bother to lock their car doors.

Since police patrols might be out along Kanackaway, hoping for the killer to return to the scene as well, a man sitting alone in a car would be highly suspicious. Chase started the engine and headed back into the city.

As he drove, he tried to recall everything that he had seen, so no clue to Judge's identity would slip by. The guy owned a silencer-equipped pistol and a red Volkswagen. He was a bad shot, but a good driver. And that was about the sum of it.

What next? The police?

No. To hell with the cops. He had sought help from Fauvel and received nothing but bad advice. The cops had been even less help.

He would have to handle the whole business himself. Track Judge down before Judge killed him.

* * *

Mrs. Fielding met him at the door but stepped backward in surprise when she saw his condition. 'What happened to you?'

'I fell down,' Chase said. 'It's nothing.'

'But there's blood on your face. You're all skinned up!'

'Really, Mrs. Fielding, I'm perfectly all right now. I had a little accident, but I'm on my feet and breathing.'

She looked him over more carefully. 'Have you been drinking, Mr. Chase?' Her tone had gone swiftly from concern to disapproval.

'No drinks at all,' Chase said.

'You know I don't approve.'

'I know.' He went past her, heading for the stairs. They appeared to be a long way off.

'You didn't wreck your car?' she called after him.

'No.'

He climbed the stairs, looking anxiously ahead toward the turn at the landing – blessed escape. Strangely, he did not feel nearly as oppressed by Mrs. Fielding as usual.

'That's good news,' she said. 'As long as you have your car, you'll be able to look for jobs better than before.'

After a glass of whiskey over ice, he drew a tub of water as hot as he could tolerate it, and he settled in as though he were an old man with arthritis. Water slopped over his open wounds and made him sigh with both pleasure and pain.

Later, he dressed the worst abrasions with Merthiolate, then put on lightweight slacks, a sports shirt, socks, and loafers. With a second glass of whiskey, he sat in the easy chair to contemplate his next move.

He looked forward to action with a mixture of excitement and apprehension.

First, he should speak with Louise Allenby, the girl who had been with Michael Karnes the night he was killed. She and Chase had been questioned separately by the police, but brooding on the event together, they might be able to remember something useful.

The telephone book listed eighteen Allenbys, but Chase recalled Louise telling Detective Wallace that her father was dead and that her mother had not remarried. Only one of the Allenbys in the book was listed as a woman: Cleta Allenby on Pine Street, an address in the Ashside district.

He dialed the number and waited through ten rings before Louise answered. Her voice was recognizable, although more womanly than he remembered.

'This is Ben Chase, Louise. Do you remember me?'

'Of course,' she said. She sounded genuinely

pleased to hear from him. 'How are you?'

'Coping.'

'What's wrong? Is there anything I can do to help?'

'I'd like to talk to you, if possible,' Chase said. 'About what happened Monday night.'

'Well, sure, all right.'

'It won't upset you?'

'Why should it?' Her hardness continued to amaze him. 'Can you come over now?'

'If it's convenient.'

'Fine,' she said. 'It's ten o'clock now – in half an hour, at ten-thirty? Will that be all right?'

'Just right,' Chase said.

'I'll be expecting you.'

She put the phone down so gently that for seconds Chase did not realize that she had hung up.

He was beginning to stiffen from his injuries. He stood and stretched, found his car keys, and quickly finished his drink.

When it was time to go, he did not want to begin. Suddenly he realized how completely this assumption of responsibility would destroy the simple routines by which he had survived in the months since his discharge from the army and the hospital. He would have no more leisurely mornings in town, no more afternoons watching old movies on television, no more evenings reading and drinking until he could sleep – at least not until this mess was straightened out. If he just stayed here in his room, however, if he took his chances, he might remain alive until Judge was caught in a few weeks or, at most, in a few months.

Then again, Judge might not miss the next time.

He cursed everyone who had forced him out of his comfortable niche – the local press, the Merchants' Association, Judge, Fauvel, Wallace, Tuppinger – yet he knew that he had no choice but to get on with it. His sole consolation was the hope that their victory was only a temporary one: When this was all finished, he would come back to this room, close the door, and settle once more into the quiet and unchallenging life that he had established for himself during the past year.

Mrs. Fielding did not bother him on his way out of the house, and he chose to see this as a good omen.

* * *

The Allenbys, mother and daughter, lived in a two-story neo-Colonial brick home on a small lot in middle-class Ashside. Two matched maples were featured at the head of the short flagstone walk and two matched pines at the end of it. Two steps rose to a white door with a brass knocker.

Louise answered the door herself. She was wearing white shorts and a thin white halter top, and she looked as if she had spent the past thirty minutes putting on makeup and brushing her long hair.

'Come in,' she said.

The living room was more or less what he had expected: matched Colonial furniture, a color television in a huge console cabinet, knotted rugs over polished pine floors. The house was not dirty but carelessly kept: magazines spilling out of a rack, a dried water ring on the coffee table, traces of dust here and there.

'Sit down,' Louise said. 'The sofa's comfortable, and so's that big chair with the flowered print.'

He chose the sofa. 'I'm sorry to bother you like this, so late at night – '

'Don't worry about that,' she interrupted breezily. 'You're no bother, never could be.'

He hardly recognized her as the shaken, whimpering girl in Michael Karnes's car on Monday night.

She said, 'Since I'm finished with school, I only go to bed when I feel like it, usually around three in the morning. College in the fall. Big girl now.' She grinned as if she'd never had a boyfriend knifed to death in front of her. 'Can I get you a drink?'

'No, thanks.'

'Mind if I have something?'

'Go ahead.'

He stared at her trim legs as she went to the wet bar in the wall of bookcases. 'Sicilian Stinger. Sure you wouldn't like one? They're delicious.'

'I'm fine.'

As she mixed the drink with professional expertise, she stood with her back to him, her hips artfully canted, her round butt thrust toward him. It might have been the unconscious stance of a girl not yet fully aware of her womanliness, with only a partial understanding of the effect her pneumatic body could have on men. Or it might have been completely contrived.

When she returned to the sofa with her drink, Chase said, 'Are you old enough to drink?'

'Seventeen,' she said. 'Almost eighteen. No longer a child, right? Maybe I'm not of legal age yet, but this is my own home, so who's going to stop me?'

'Of course.'

Only seven years ago, when he'd been her age, seventeen-year-old girls *seemed* seventeen. They grew up faster now – or thought they did.

Sipping her drink, she leaned back against the couch and crossed her bare legs.

He saw the hard tips of her breasts against the thin halter.

He said, 'It's just occurred to me that your

mother may be in bed, if she gets up early for work. I didn't mean – '

'Mother's working now,' Louise said. She looked at him coyly, her lashes lowered and her head tilted to one side. 'She's a cocktail waitress. She goes on duty at seven, off at three, home about three-thirty in the morning.'

'I see.'

'Are you frightened?'

'Excuse me?'

She smiled mischievously. 'Of being here alone with me?'

'No.'

'Good. So . . . where do we begin?' With another coy look, she tried to make the question seductive.

For the following half hour, he guided her through her memories of Monday night, augmenting them with his own, questioning her on details, urging her to question him, looking for some small thing that might be the key. They remembered nothing new, however, though the girl genuinely tried to help him. She was able to talk about Mike Karnes's murder with complete detachment, as though she had not been there when it happened but had only read about it in the papers.

'Mind if I have another one?' she asked, raising her glass.

'Go ahead.'

'I'm feeling good. Want one this time?'

'No, thank you,' he said, recognizing the need to keep his head clear.

She stood at the wet bar in the same provocative pose as before, and when she returned to the couch, she sat much closer to him than she had previously. 'One thing I just thought of – he was wearing a special ring.'

'Special in what way?'

'Silver, squarish, with a double lightning bolt. A guy Mom dated for a while wore one. I asked him about it once, and he told me it was a brotherhood ring, from this club he belonged to.'

'What club?'

'Just for white guys. No blacks, Japs, Jews, or anybody else welcome, just white guys.'

Chase waited as she sipped her drink.

'Bunch of guys who're willing to stand up for themselves, if it ever comes to that, guys who aren't going to let the nappy-heads or the Jew bankers or anybody else push them around and take what they have.' She clearly approved of any such organization. Then she frowned. 'Did I just screw up my chances?'

'Chances?'

'Are you maybe a Jew?'

'No.'

'You don't look like a Jew.'

'I'm not.'

'Listen, even if you were a Jew, it wouldn't matter much to me. I find you real attractive. You know?'

'So the killer might be a white supremacist?'

'They're just guys who won't take any crap the way everyone else will. That's all. You have to admire that.'

'This guy who dated your mother – did he tell you the name of this club?'

'The Aryan Alliance.'

'You remember his name?'

'Vic. Victor. Don't remember his last name.'

'Could you ask your mom for me?'

'Okay. When she gets home. Listen, you're absolutely sure you're not a Jew?'

'I'm sure.'

'Because ever since I said it, you've been looking at me sort of funny.'

As he might have looked at something pale and squirming that he'd discovered under an overturned rock.

He said, 'Did you tell Wallace about this?'

'No, I just now thought of it. You loosened me up, and it just came back to me in a flash.'

Chase imagined nothing more gratifying than establishing a body of information about Judge – working from this essential bit of data – and then presenting it to the detective.

'It may be helpful,' he said.

She slid next to him with the oiled smoothness of a machine made for seduction, all sleek lines and golden tan. 'Do you think so, Ben?'

He nodded, trying to decide how best to excuse himself without hurting her feelings. He had to keep on the good side of her until she got that name from her mother.

Her thigh was pressed against his. She put her drink down and turned to him, expecting to be embraced.

Chase stood abruptly. 'I ought to be going. This has given me something concrete to consider, more than I had hoped for.'

She rose too, remaining close to him. 'It's early. Not even midnight. Mom won't be home for hours.'

She smelled of soap, shampoo, a pleasant perfume. It was such a clean smell – but he knew now that she was corrupted in her heart.

He was fiercely aroused – and sickened by his arousal. This cheap, cold-hearted, hate-filled girl reached him in a way that no woman had reached him in longer than a year, and he despised himself for wanting her so intensely. At that moment, of course, virtually any attractive woman might have affected him the same way. Perhaps the pent-up sexual energy of many lonely months had become too great to repress, and perhaps the reawakening of sexual desire was the result of being forced out of his self-imposed isolation. Once he admitted to a healthy survival instinct, once he decided not to stand still and be a target for Judge, he was able to admit to all the desires and needs that were the essence of life. Nevertheless, he despised himself.

'No,' he said, edging away from her. 'I have other people to see.'

'At this hour?'

'One or two other people.'

She pressed against him, pulled his face down to hers, and licked his lips. No kiss. Just the maddeningly quick flicking of her warm tongue – an exquisitely erotic promise.

'We've got the house for several hours yet,' she said. 'We don't even have to use the couch. I've got a great big white bed with a white canopy.'

'You're something else,' he said, meaning something other than what she thought he meant.

'You don't know the half of it,' she said.

'But I can't. I really can't, because these people are waiting for me.'

She was experienced enough to know when the moment for seduction had passed. She stepped back and smiled. 'But I do want to thank you. For saving my life. That deserves a big reward.'

'You don't owe me anything,' he said.

'I *do*. Some other night, when you don't have plans?'

He kissed her, telling himself that he did so only to remain in her good graces. 'Definitely some other night.'

'Mmmmm. And we'll be good together.'

She was all polish, fast and easy, no jagged edges to get hung up on.

He said, 'If Detective Wallace questions you again, do you think you could sort of . . . forget about the ring?'

'Sure. I don't like cops. They're the ones who put the guns to our heads, make us kiss the asses of the nappy-heads and the Jews and all of them. They're part of the problem. But why are you carrying on with this by yourself? I never did ask.'

'Personal,' he said. 'For personal reasons.'

* * *

At home again, he undressed and went directly to bed. The darkness was heavy and warm and, for the first time in longer than he could remember, comforting.

Alone, he began to wonder if he had been a fool not to respond to Louise Allenby's offer. He had been a long time without a woman, without even a desire for one.

He had told himself that he'd rejected Louise because he'd found her as personally repulsive as she was physically attractive. But he wondered if, instead, he'd retreated from the prospect because he feared it would draw him even further into the world, further away from his precious routines. A relationship with a woman, regardless of how transitory, would be one more crack in his carefully mortared walls.

On the edge of sleep, he realized that something had happened that was far more important than either his strong physical response to Louise or his rejection of her. For the first time in longer than Chase could recall, he hadn't needed whiskey before bed. A natural sleep claimed him – although it was still populated by the grasping dead.

8

When he woke in the morning, Chase was racked with pain from the fall that he had taken the previous evening on Kanackaway Ridge Road. Each contusion and laceration throbbed. His eyes felt sunken, and his headache was as intense as if he'd been fitted with an exotic torture device – an iron helmet – that would be slowly tightened until his skull imploded. When he tried to get out of bed, his muscles cramped and spasmed.

In the bathroom, when he leaned toward the mirror above the sink, he saw that he was drawn and pale. His chest and back were spotted with bruises, most about as large as a thumbprint, from the gravel over which he'd rolled to avoid the hurtling truck.

A hot bath didn't soothe him, so he forced himself to do a couple of dozen situps, pushups, and deep knee bends until he was dizzy. The exercises proved more therapeutic than the bath.

The only cure for his misery was activity – which, he supposed, was a prescription for his emotional and spiritual miseries as well.

Wincing at the pain in his legs, he went downstairs.

'Mail for you,' said Mrs. Fielding as she shuffled out of the game-show-audience laughter in the living room. She took a plain brown envelope from the table in the hall and gave it to him. 'As you can see, there's no return address.'

'Probably advertisements,' Chase said. He took a step toward the front door, hoping that she wouldn't notice his stiffness and inquire about his health.

He need not have worried, because she was more interested in the contents of the envelope than in him. 'It can't be an ad in a plain envelope. The only things that come in plain envelopes without return addresses are wedding invitations – which this isn't – and dirty literature.' Her expression was uncharacteristically stern. 'I won't tolerate dirty literature in my house.'

'And I don't blame you,' Chase said.

'Then it isn't?'

'No.' He opened the envelope and withdrew the psychiatric file and journal articles that Judge had promised to send to him. 'I'm interested in psychology, and this friend of mine sometimes sends me particularly interesting articles on the subject when he comes across them.'

'Oh.' Mrs. Fielding was obviously surprised that Chase harbored such intellectual and hitherto unknown interests. 'Well ... I hope I didn't embarrass you – '

'Not at all.'

' – but I couldn't tolerate having pornography in my home.'

Barely refraining from commenting on the half-undone bodice of her housedress, he said, 'I understand.'

He went out to his car and drove three blocks before pulling to the curb. Letting the engine idle, he examined the Xeroxes.

The extensive handwritten notes that Dr. Fauvel had made during their session were so difficult to read that Chase passed over them for the time being, but he studied the five articles – three in the form of magazine tearsheets, two in typescript. In all five pieces, Fauvel's high self-esteem was evident, his egotism unrelenting. The doctor referred to the subject as 'Patient C'; however, Chase recognised himself – even though he was portrayed through a radically distorting lens. Every symptom that he suffered had been exaggerated to make its eventual amelioration appear to be a greater achievement on Fauvel's part. All the clumsy probes that Fauvel had initiated were never mentioned, and he claimed to have succeeded with strategies of therapy that he'd never employed but that he'd apparently developed through hindsight. Chase was, according to Fauvel: *one of those young men who go to war with no well-formed moral beliefs and who, therefore, are clay in the hands of manipulative superiors, capable of being induced to commit any atrocities without questioning their orders.* Elsewhere, he observed that Patient C: *came to me from a military hospital, where he had recovered sufficiently from a total nervous breakdown to attempt social reintegration. The cause of his breakdown had been not a sense of guilt but extreme terror at the prospect of his own death, not a concern for others but crippling recognition – and fear – of his own mortality.*

'You bastard,' Chase said. Guilt had been his constant companion, whether he was awake or asleep. Recognition of his mortality had not been a source of fear, for God's sake; instead, it had been his only consolation, and for a long time he had hoped for nothing more than the strength to end his own life.

Fauvel had written: *He still suffered nightmares and impotence, which he felt were his only afflictions and were a result of his fear. I recognized, however, that the real problem for Patient C was an underlying lack of moral values. He could never heal himself psychologically until he made peace with his horrific past, and he could not make peace with his past until he fully understood and acknowledged the gravity of the crimes that he had committed, even if in war.*

Understood and acknowledged! As if Chase had blithely pulled the trigger, waded through the blood of his victims, and then had gone in search of a good shoeshine boy to buff the stains off his boots. Jesus.

Dr. G. Sloan Fauvel – psychiatrist extraordinaire, confessor, and tower of moral rectitude – had therefore: *at last commenced the long, difficult process of inculcating in Patient C, by diverse and subtle means, an understanding of the concept of morality and a capacity for guilt. If he could develop a sincere sense of guilt about what he had done, then the guilt subsequently could be relieved through classic therapy. A cure might then be possible.*

Chase returned the material to the plain brown envelope. He tucked the envelope under the passenger seat.

He was shaken by the realization that he had spent so much time in the care of a physician who neither understood him nor possessed the capacity to understand. For too long, Chase had trusted in others to save him, but the only salvation was to be found in God and in himself.

And after his experience in Southeast Asia, he still was not entirely sure of God.

* * *

In the Metropolitan Bureau of Vital Statistics, in the basement of the courthouse, three women hammered away at typewriters with a rhythmic swiftness that seemed to have been arranged and conducted with all the care of a symphony-orchestra performance.

Chase stood at the reception counter, waiting for service.

The stoutest and oldest of the three women – her desk plate read NANCY ONUFER, *Manager* – typed to the end of a page, pulled the page from her typewriter, and placed it in a clear-plastic tray full of similar forms. 'May I help you?'

He had already figured what tact Judge must have used when asking to search the files here, and he said, 'I'm doing a family history, and I was wondering if I could be permitted to look up a few things in the city records.'

'Certainly,' said Nancy Onufer. She popped up from her chair, came to the gate at the end of the service counter, and opened it for him.

The other two women continued to type with machine-gun rapidity. There was a high degree of efficiency in the Bureau of Statistics that was unusual for any government office, no doubt because Nancy Onufer would accept no less. Her brisk but not unfriendly manner reminded Chase of the better drill sergeants whom he had known in the service.

He followed her through the office area behind the counter, past desks and worktables, and through a fire door into a large concrete-walled chamber lined with metal filing cabinets. More cabinets stood in rows down the center of the room, and to one side was a scarred worktable with three hard chairs.

'The cabinets are all labeled,' Nancy Onufer said crisply. 'The section to the right contains birth certificates, death certificates there, then health-department records over there, bar and restaurant licenses in that corner. Against the far wall we keep carbons of the draft-board records, then the minutes and budgets of the city council going back thirty years. You get the idea. Depending on the contents, each drawer is primarily organized either alphabetically or by date. Whatever you remove from the files must be left on this table. Do not attempt to replace the material yourself. That's my job, and I do it far more accurately than you would. No offense.'

'None taken.'

'You may not remove anything from this room.

For a nominal fee, one of my assistants will provide photocopies of documents that interest you. If anything should be removed from this room, you will be subjected to a five-thousand-dollar fine and two years in prison.'

'Ouch.'

'We enforce it too.'

'I've no doubt. Thanks for your help.'

'And no smoking,' she added.

'I don't.'

'Good.'

She left the room, closing the door behind her.

It had been this easy for Judge too. Chase had hoped that the city would require a sign-in procedure by which those who wanted to use the files were identified. Considering Nancy Onufer's efficiency and the law against removing documents, Chase was surprised that she didn't keep a meticulous log of visitors.

He looked up his own birth certificate and also found the minutes of the city-council meeting during which a vote had been taken to hold an awards dinner in his honor. In the carbons of the selective-service records, he located the pertinent facts regarding his past eligibility for the draft and the document calling him for service in the United States Army.

Easy. Too easy.

When he left the storage vault, Nancy Onufer

said, 'Find what you were looking for?'

'Yes, thank you.'

'No trouble, Mr. Chase,' she said, immediately turning back to her work.

Her reply stopped him. 'You know me?'

She glanced up and flashed a smile. 'Who doesn't?'

He crossed the open office area to her desk. 'If you hadn't known who I was, would you have asked for a name and ID before I went into the file room?'

'Certainly. No one's ever taken any records in the twelve years I've been here, but I still keep a log of visitors.' She tapped a notebook on the edge of her desk. 'I just put your name down.'

'This may sound like an odd request, but could you tell me who was here this past Tuesday?' When Mrs. Onufer hesitated, he said, 'I'm being bothered by a lot of reporters, and I don't care for all the publicity. They've said everything about me there is to be said, after all. It's getting to be overkill. I've heard there's a local man working on a series for a national magazine, against my wishes, and I was wondering if he'd been here Tuesday.'

He thought that the lie was transparent, but she trusted him. He was a war hero, after all. 'It must be a pain in the butt. But journalists – they can never leave anyone alone. Anyway, I don't see the harm in telling you who was here. There's nothing confidential about the visitors' log.' She consulted the notebook. 'Only nine people came around all Tuesday. These two are from an architectural firm, checking some power-and-water easements on properties they're developing. I know them. These four were women, and you're looking for a man, so we can rule them out. That leaves three – here, here, and here.'

As she showed him the names, Chase tried to commit them to memory. 'No . . . I guess . . . none of them is him.'

'Anything else?'

'Do you ordinarily just take names – or ask for ID?'

'Always ID, unless I know the person.'

'Well, thanks for your help.'

Acutely conscious of all the work on her desk, Nancy Onufer shut the notebook, dismissed Chase with a quick smile, and returned to her typing.

When he left the courthouse, it was a quarter till noon, and he was starving. He went to a drive-in restaurant – Diamond Dell – that had been a favorite hangout when he'd been in high school.

He was surprised by his appetite. Sitting in the car, he ate two cheeseburgers, a large order of fries, and cole slaw, washing it all down with a Pepsi. That was more than he had eaten in any *three* meals during the past year.

After lunch, at a nearby service station, he used the phonebooth directory to find numbers for the men who were possibles in Nancy Onufer's log. When he called the first, he got the guy's wife; she gave him a work number for her husband. Chase dialed it and spoke to the suspect – who sounded nothing whatsoever like Judge. The second man was at home, and he sounded even less like Judge than the first.

The directory had no number for the third man – Howard Devore – which might only mean that his telephone was unlisted. Or it might mean that the name was phony. Of course, Mrs. Onufer always asked for ID, so if Judge was using a phony name, he also must have access to a source of false identification.

Because he didn't trust himself to remember every clue and to notice links between them, Chase went to a drugstore and purchased a small ring-bound notebook and a Bic pen. Inspired by Mrs. Onufer's efficiency, he made a neat list:

Alias – Judge
Alias – Howard Devore (possible)
Aryan Alliance
No criminal record (prints not on file)

Can pick locks (Fauvel's office)
May own a red Volkswagen
Owns a pistol with sound suppressor

Sitting in his car in the drugstore parking lot, he studied the list for a while, then added another item:

Unemployed or on vacation

He could think of no other way to explain how Judge could call him at any hour, follow him in the middle of the afternoon, and spend two days researching his life. The killer neither sounded nor acted old enough to be retired. Unemployed, on vacation – or on a leave of absence from his work.

But how could that information be useful in finding the bastard? It narrowed the field of suspects but not significantly. The local economy was bad; therefore, more than a few people were out of work. And it was summer, vacation season.

He closed the notebook and started the car. He was dead serious about tracking down Judge, but he felt less like Sam Spade than like Nancy Drew.

* * *

Glenda Kleaver, the young blonde in charge of the *Press-Dispatch* morgue room, was about five feet eleven, only two inches shorter than Chase. In spite of her size, her voice was as soft as the July breeze that lazily stirred maple-leaf shadows across the sun-gilded windows. She moved with natural grace, and Chase was instantly fascinated with her, not solely because of her quiet beauty but because she seemed to calm the world around her by her very presence.

She demonstrated the use of microfilm viewers to Chase and explained that all editions prior to January 1, 1968, were now stored on film to conserve space. She explained the procedure for ordering the proper spools and for obtaining the editions that had not yet been transferred to film.

Two reporters were sitting at the machines, twisting the controls, staring into the viewers, jotting on notepads beside them.

Chase said, 'Do you get many outsiders here?'

'A newspaper morgue is chiefly for the use of the staff. But we keep it open to the public without charge. We get maybe a dozen people a week.'

'What are outsiders looking for here?'

'What are *you* looking for?' she asked.

He hesitated, then gave her the same story that he had first given Mrs. Onufer at the Metropolitan Bureau of Vital Statistics. 'I'm gathering facts for a family history.'

'That's what most outsiders come here for. Personally, I haven't the least bit of curiosity about dead relatives. I don't even like the living relatives very much.'

He laughed, surprised to discover acidic humor in someone so gentle-looking and so soft-spoken. She was a study in contrasts. 'No sense of pride in your lineage?'

'None,' she said. 'It's more mutt than thoroughbred.'

'Nothing wrong with that.'

'Go back far enough in my family tree,' she said, 'and I bet you'll find some ancestors hanging from the limbs by their necks.'

'Descended from horse thieves, huh?'

'At best.'

Chase was more at ease with her than he had been in the presence of any woman since Jules Verne, the underground operation in Nam. But when it came to small talk, he was long out of practice, and as much as he would have liked to make a stronger connection with her, he was unable to think of anything to say except: 'Well ... do I have to sign anything to use the files?'

'No. But I have to get everything for you, and you have to return it to me before you leave. What do you need?'

Chase had come there not to conduct research

but only to ask about any outsiders who had
used the morgue this past Tuesday, but no convenient cover story came to mind. He could not
spin the same tale that he'd used with Mrs.
Onufer, the lie about the nosy reporter – not here
of all places.

Furthermore, though he had been prepared to
make up any story that circumstances seemed
to require, he discovered that he didn't want to
lie to this woman. Her blue-gray eyes were
direct, and in them he saw a forthrightness and
honesty that he was compelled to respect.

On the other hand, if he told her the truth
about Judge and the attempt on his life, and if
she didn't believe him, he would feel like a prize
ass. Oddly enough, although he had only just
met her, he didn't want to embarrass himself in
front of her.

Besides, one of the reporters working in the
morgue might overhear too much. Then Chase's
picture would be on the front page again. They
might treat the story either straight or tongue-
in-cheek (probably the latter, if they talked to
the police), but either way the publicity would
be an intolerable development.

'Sir?' Glenda said. 'How can I help you? What
editions would you like to see first?'

Before Chase could respond, a reporter at one
of the mircrofilm machines looked up from his

work. 'Glenda, dear, could I have all the dailies between May 15, 1952, and September that same year?'

'In a moment. This gentleman was first.'

'That's okay,' Chase said, grasping the opportunity. 'I've got plenty of time.'

'You sure?' she asked.

'Yeah. Get him what he needs.'

'I'll be back in five minutes,' she said.

As she walked the length of the small room and through the wide arch into the filing room, both Chase and the reporter watched her. She was tall but not awkward, moving with a feline grace that actually made her seem fragile.

When she had gone, the reporter said, 'Thanks for waiting.'

'Sure.'

'I've got an eleven o'clock deadline on this piece, and I haven't even begun to get my sources together.' He turned back to his viewer, so engrossed in his work that he apparently had not recognized Chase.

Chase returned to his Mustang, opened his notebook, and studied his list, but he had absolutely nothing to add to it, and he could not see any pertinent connections between the familiar eight items. He closed the book, started the car, and drove out into the traffic on John F. Kennedy Throughway.

Fifteen minutes later he was on the four-lane interstate beyond the city limits, doing a steady seventy miles an hour, wind whistling at the open windows and ruffling his hair. As he drove, he thought about Glenda Kleaver, and he hardly noticed the miles going by.

* * *

After high school Chase had gone to State because it was just forty miles from home, so he could see his mom and dad more often, still get back to visit old friends from high school and to see a girl who had mattered to him them, before Vietnam changed everything.

Now, as he parked in front of the administration building, the campus seemed to be a strange place, as if he had not spent nearly four years in these classrooms, on these flagstone paths, under these canopies of willows and elms. This part of his life was all but lost to him because it was from the far side of the war. To recapture the mood and feeling of that time, to connect emotionally with these old haunts, he would have to cross through the river of war memories to the shores of the past – and that was a journey that he chose not to make.

In the Student Records Office, as the manager approached him, Chase decided that this time the simple truth would get the best response. 'I'm curious to know who may have been here, asking about me, within the past week. I'm having some problems with a researcher who's . . . well, been more or less harassing me.'

The manager was a small, pale, nervous man with a neatly clipped mustache. He ceaselessly picked up items around him, put them down, picked them up again: pencils, pens, a notepad, a pamphlet about the university's tuition schedules and scholarship programs. He said that his name was Franklin Brown and that he was pleased to meet such a distinguished alumnus. 'But there must've been dozens of inquiries about you in recent months, Mr. Chase, ever since the Medal of Honor was announced.'

'Do you have the names and addresses of everyone requesting records?'

'Oh, yes, of course. And as you may know, we provide those records only to prospective employers – and even then only if you signed an automatic authorization when you graduated.'

'This man may have passed himself off as a prospective employer. He's very convincing. Could you check your records and tell me who might have stopped in last Tuesday?'

'He could have requested the records by mail. Most of the inquiries we receive are by mail. Few people actually come in.'

'No. He didn't have time to do it by mail.'

'Just a moment then,' Brown said. He brought a ledger to the counter and thumbed through it. 'There was just the one gentleman that day.'

'Who was he?'

As he read it, Brown showed the entry to Chase. 'Eric Blentz, Gateway Mall Tavern. It's in the city.'

'I know exactly where it's at,' Chase said.

Picking up a fountain pen, twisting it in his fingers, putting it down again, Brown asked, 'Is he legitimate? Is he someone you're seeking a position with?'

'No. It's probably this reporter I mentioned, and he just made up the name Blentz. Do you remember what he looked like?'

'Certainly,' Brown said. 'Nearly your height, though not robust at all, very thin, in fact, and with a stoop to his shoulders.'

'How old?'

'Thirty-eight, forty.'

'His face? Do you remember that?'

'Very ascetic features,' Brown said. 'Very quick eyes. He kept looking from one of my girls here to the other, then at me, as if he didn't trust us. His cheeks were drawn, an unhealthy complexion. A large thin nose, so thin the nostrils were very elliptical.'

'Hair?'

'Blond. He was quite sharp with me, impatient, self-important. Dressed very neatly, a high polish to his shoes. I don't think there was a hair out of place on his head. And when I asked for his name and business address, he took the pen right out of my hand, turned the ledger around, and wrote it down himself because, as he said, everyone always spelled his name wrong, and he wanted it right this time.'

Chase said, 'How is it that you remember him in such detail?'

Brown smiled, picked up the pen, put it down, and toyed with the ledger as he said, 'Evenings and weekends during the summer, my wife and I run The Footlight. It's a legitimate theater in town – you might even have attended a play there when you were in school. Anyway, I take a role in most of our productions, so I'm always studying people to pick up expressions, mannerisms.'

'You must be very good on stage by now,' Chase said.

Brown blushed. 'Not particularly. But that kind of thing gets in your blood. We don't make much money on the theater, but as long as it breaks even, I can indulge myself.'

Returning to his car, Chase tried to picture Franklin Brown on stage, before an audience, his hands trembling, his face paler than ever; his

compulsion to handle things might be exacer-
bated by being in the spotlight. Perhaps it was
no mystery why The Footlight didn't show much
profit.

In the Mustang, Chase opened his notebook
and looked over the list that he'd made earlier,
trying to find something that indicated Judge
might actually be Eric Blentz, a saloon owner.
No good. Didn't anyone who applied for a liquor
license have to be finger-printed as a matter of
routine? And a man who owned a thriving business like the Gateway Mall Tavern probably
wouldn't drive a Volkswagen.

There was one way to find out for sure. He
started the car and drove back toward the city,
wondering what sort of reception he would get
at the Gateway Mall Tavern.

9

The tavern decor was supposed to be reminiscent of an alpine inn: low-beamed ceilings, rough white plaster walls, a brick floor, heavy dark-pine furniture. The six windows that faced onto the mall promenade were leaded glass the color of burgundy, only slightly translucent. Around the walls were upholstered booths. Chase sat in one of the smaller booths toward the rear of the place, facing the bar and the front entrance.

A cheerful apple-cheeked blonde in a short brown skirt and low-cut white peasant blouse lit the lantern on his table, then took his order for a whiskey sour.

The bar was not especially busy at six o'clock; only seven other patrons shared the place, three couples and a lone woman who sat at the bar. None of the customers fit the description that Brown had given Chase, and he disregarded them. The bartender was the only other man in the place, aging and bald, with a potbelly, but quick and expert with the bottles and obviously a favorite with barmaids.

Blentz might not frequent his own tavern, of course, though he would be an exception to the rule if that was the case. This was largely a cash business, and most saloon owners liked to keep a watch on the till.

Chase realized that he was tense, leaning away from the back of the booth, his hands curled into fists on the table. He settled back and forced himself to relax, since he might have to wait hours for Blentz.

After the second whiskey sour, he asked for a menu and ordered a veal chop and a baked potato, surprised to be hungry after the meal that he'd had at the drive-in joint earlier.

After dinner, shortly after nine o'clock, Chase finally asked the waitress if Mr. Blentz would be in this evening.

She looked across the now-crowded room and pointed at a heavy-set man on a stool at the bar. 'That's him.'

The guy was about fifty, weighed well over two hundred and fifty pounds, and was four or five inches shorter than the man in Franklin Brown's description.

'Blentz?' Chase asked. 'You're sure?'

'I've worked for him for two years,' the waitress said.

'I was told he was tall, thin. Blond hair, sharp dresser.'

'Maybe twenty years ago he was thin and a sharp dresser,' she said. 'But he couldn't ever have been tall or blond.'

'I guess not,' Chase said. 'I guess I must be looking for another Blentz. Could I have the bill, please?'

He felt like Nancy Drew again, rather than Sam Spade. Of course, Nancy Drew *did* solve every case – and generally, if not always, before anyone was killed.

When he went outside, the mall parking lot was deserted but for the cars in front of the tavern. The stores had closed twenty minutes before.

The night air was sultry after the air-conditioned tavern. It seemed to press Chase to the blacktop, so each step that he took was flat-footed, loud, as though he were walking on a planet with greater gravity than that of earth.

As he was wiping sweat from his forehead, stepping around the front of the Mustang, he heard an engine roar behind him and was pinned by headlights. He didn't turn to look, but vaulted out of the way and onto the hood of his car.

An instant later a Pontiac scraped noisily along the side of the Mustang. Showers of sparks briefly brightened the night, leaving behind a faint smell of hot metal and scorched paint.

Although the car rocked hard when it was struck, Chase held fast by curling his fingers into the trough that housed the recessed windshield wipers. If he fell off, the Pontiac sure as hell would swing around or back up to run him down before he could scramble away again.

Chase stood on the hood of the Mustang and stared after the retreating Pontiac, trying to see the license number. Even if he had been close enough to read the dark numerals, he couldn't have done so, because Judge had twisted a large piece of burlap sacking over the plate.

The Pontiac reached the exit lane from the mall lot, took the turn too hard, and appeared in danger of shooting across the sidewalk and striking one of the mercury arc lights. But then Judge regained control, accelerated, went through the amber traffic light at the intersection, and swung right onto the main highway toward the heart of the city. In seconds, the Pontiac passed over the brow of a hill and was out of sight.

Chase looked around to see if anyone had witnessed the short, violent confrontation. He was alone.

He got down from the hood and walked the length of the Mustang, examining the damage. The front fender was jammed back toward the driver's door, though it hadn't been crushed against the tire and wouldn't prevent the car from being driven. The entire flank of the vehicle was scraped and crumpled. He doubted that there was any serious structural or mechanical damage – although the body work would cost several hundred bucks to repair.

He didn't care. Money was the least of his worries.

He opened the driver's door, which protested with only a thin shriek, sat behind the wheel, closed the door, opened his notebook, and reread his list. His hand trembled when he added the ninth, tenth, and eleventh items:

Third alias – Eric Blentz
Given to rash action in the face of previous
    failures
Pontiac, second car (stolen just to make the
    hit?)

He sat in the car, staring at the empty lot, until his hands stopped shaking. Weary, he drove home, wondering where Judge would be waiting for him the next time.

* * *

The telephone woke him Saturday morning.

Rising from a darkness full of accusatory

corpses, Chase put a hand on the receiver – then realized who might be calling. Judge hadn't phone since early Wednesday night. He was overdue.

'Hello?'

'Ben?'

'Yes?'

'Dr. Fauvel here.'

It was the first time that Chase had ever heard the psychiatrist on the phone. Except during their office sessions, all communications were through Miss Pringle.

'What do you want?' Chase asked. The name had fully awakened him and chased off his lingering nightmares.

'I wondered why you hadn't kept your Friday appointment.'

'Didn't need it.'

Fauvel hesitated. Then: 'Listen, if it was because I talked to the police so frankly, you must understand that I wasn't violating a doctor-patient relationship. They weren't accusing you of any crime, and I thought it was in your best interest to tell them the truth before they wasted more time on this Judge.'

Chase said nothing.

Fauvel said, 'Should we get together this afternoon and talk about it, all of it?'

'No.'

'I think you would benefit from a session right now, Ben.'

'I'm not coming in again.'

'That would be unwise,' Fauvel said.

'Psychiatric care was not a condition of my hospital discharge, only a benefit I could avail myself of.'

'And you still *can* avail yourself of it, Ben. I'm here, waiting to see you –'

'It's no longer a benefit,' Chase said. He was beginning to enjoy this. For the first time, he had Fauvel on the defensive for more than a brief moment; the new balance of power was gratifying.

'Ben, you *are* angry about what I said to the police. That is the whole thing, isn't it?'

'Partly,' Chase said. 'But there are other reasons.'

'What?'

Chase said, 'Let's play the word-association game.'

'Word association? Ben, don't be –'

'Publish.'

'Ben, I'm ready to see you any time that –'

'Publish,' Chase interrupted.

'This doesn't help –'

'Publish,' Chase insisted.

Fauvel was silent. Then he sighed, decided to play along, and said, 'I guess . . . books.'

'Magazines.'

'I don't know where you want me to go, Ben.'

'Magazines.'

'Well . . . newspapers.'

'Magazines.'

'New word, please,' Fauvel said.

'Contents.'

'Oh. Articles?'

'Five.'

'Five articles?'

'Psychiatry.'

Puzzled, Fauvel said, 'You're not managing this correctly. Word association has to be –'

'Patient C.'

Fauvel was stunned into silence.

'Patient C,' Chase repeated.

'How did you get hold of –'

'One word.'

'Ben, we can't discuss this in one-word exchanges. I'm sure you're upset, but –'

'Play the game with me, Doctor, and maybe – just maybe – I won't make a public response to your five articles and won't subject you to professional ridicule.'

The silence on the other end of the line was as deep as any Chase had ever heard.

'Patient C,' Chase said.

'Valued.'

'Bullshit.'

'Valued,' Fauvel insisted.

'Exploited.'

'Mistake,' Fauvel admitted.

'Correction?'

'Necessary.'

'Next?'

'Session.'

'Next?'

'Session.'

'Please don't repeat your answers,' Chase admonished. 'New word – Psychiatrist.'

'Healer.'

'Psychiatrist.'

'Me.'

'Sonofabitch.'

'That's childish, Ben.'

'Egomaniac.'

Fauvel only sighed.

'Asshole,' Ben said, and he hung up.

He hadn't felt so good in years.

Later, as he was exercising the stiffness out of his battered muscles, he realized that making the break with his psychiatrist was a stronger rejection of his recent despair than anything else that he had done. He'd been telling himself that when Judge was located and dealt with, he could then resume his sheltered existence on the third floor of Mrs. Fielding's house. But that was no longer possible. By discontinuing all psychiatric treatment, he was admitting that he had changed forever and that his burden of guilt was growing distinctly less heavy.

Chase's pleasure in Fauvel's humiliation was tempered by the daunting prospect of having to *live* again. If he forsook the solace of solitude – what would replace it?

A new, quiet, but profound anxiety overcame him. Embracing the possibility of hope was far riskier and more frightening than walking boldly through enemy gunfire.

* * *

Once Chase had shaved and bathed, he realized that he had no leads to follow in his investigation. He had been everywhere that Judge had been, and yet he had gained nothing for his trouble except a description of the man, which would do him no good unless he could connect a name with it.

While eating a late breakfast at a pancake house on Galasio Boulevard, he decided to return to the Gateway Mall Tavern and talk to the real Eric Blentz to see if the man could put a name to Judge's description. It seemed likely that Judge had not just chosen Blentz's name out of the phone book when he'd used it in the Student Records Office at State. Perhaps he knew Blentz. And even if Blentz could provide no new lead, Chase could go back to Glenda Kleaver at the newspaper morgue and question her about anyone who had come into her office on Tuesday – which he hadn't done previously, for fear of making a fool of himself or pricking the interest of the reporters in the room.

From a phone booth outside the restaurant, he called the newspaper morgue, but it wasn't open for business on Saturday. In the directory he found a listing for Glenda Kleaver.

She answered on the fourth ring. He had forgotten how like music her voice was.

He said, 'Miss Kleaver, you probably don't remember me. I was in your office yesterday. My name's Chase. I had to leave while you were out of the room getting information for one of your reporters.'

'Sure. I remember you.'

He hesitated, not certain how to proceed. Then he blurted out a request or an invitation; he wasn't sure which it was. 'My name's Chase, Benjamin Chase, and I'd like to see you again, see you today, if that's at all possible.'

'See me?'

'Yes, that's right.'

After a hesitation, she said, 'Mr. Chase . . . are you asking me for a date?'

He was so out of practice – and so surprised to discover that he did, indeed, want to see her again for reasons that had nothing to do with Judge – that he was as awkward as a schoolboy.

'Well, yes, more or less, I suppose, yeah, a date, if that's okay.'

'You have an interesting approach,' she said.

'I guess so.' He was afraid that she would turn him down – and was simultaneously frightened that she would accept.

'What time?' she asked.

'Well, actually, I was thinking today, this evening, dinner.'

She was silent.

'But now,' he said, 'I realize that isn't much notice – '

'It's fine.'

'Really?' His throat was tight, and his voice rose toward an adolescent pitch. He amazed himself.

'One problem, though,' she said.

'What's that?'

'I've already started marinating a lovely sea bass for dinner. Started preparing other dishes too. I don't like wasting any of this. Could you come here for supper?'

'Okay,' he said.

She gave him the address. 'Dress casually, please. And I'll see you at seven.'

'At seven.'

When the connection was broken, Chase stood for a while in the booth, trembling. Into his mind's eye came vivid memories of Operation

Jules Verne: the narrow tunnel, the descent, the awful darkness, the fear, the bamboo gate, the women, the guns . . . the blood. His knees felt weak, and his heart beat rabbit-fast, as it had done in that subterranean battleground. Shaking violently, he leaned against the Plexiglas wall of the booth and closed his eyes.

Making a date with Glenda Kleaver was in no way a rejection of his responsibility in the deaths of those Vietnamese women. A long time had passed, after all, and a great deal of penitence had been suffered. And suffered alone.

Nevertheless, he still felt that making a date with her was wrong. Callous and selfish and wrong.

He left the booth.

The day was hot and humid. His damp shirt clung to him nearly as tenaciously as guilt.

* * *

At the shopping mall, Chase browsed in the bookstore until shortly after noon, then walked up the carpeted slope of the main promenade to the tavern. The bartender said that Blentz was expected at one o'clock. Chase sat on a stool at the bar, watching the door, and nursed a beer while he waited.

When Eric Blentz arrived, wearing a rumpled

white linen suit and a pale-yellow shirt, looking even heavier than he had appeared the previous night, he was friendly and willing to chat.

'I'm looking for a guy who used to come here,' Chase said.

Blentz overwhelmed a bar stool and ordered a beer. He listened to the description but claimed that he didn't know anyone who fit it.

'He might not have been a customer. Maybe an employee.'

'Not here, he wasn't. What do you want him for, anyway? He owe you some money?'

'Just the opposite,' Chase said. 'I owe him.'

'Yeah? How much?'

'Two hundred bucks,' Chase lied. 'You still don't know him?'

'Nope. Sorry.'

Disappointed, Chase got up. 'Thanks anyway.'

Blentz turned on his stool. 'How did you go about borrowing two hundred bucks from a guy without learning his name?'

Chase said, 'We were both drunk. If I'd been half sober, I'd have remembered it.'

Blentz smiled. 'And if he'd been half sober, he wouldn't have made the loan.'

'Probably not.'

Blentz raised his glass and took a swallow of beer. Light sparkled on the polished edges of his silver ring. A double lightning bolt.

As Chase walked across the tavern and out the door into the mall, he knew that Eric Blentz was still twisted away from the bar, watching.

Aryan Alliance. Some sort of club, like the Elks Club or the Moose Lodge, for God's sake, but for a bunch of white supremacists who had perhaps grown tired of running around the countryside in hooded white sheets and were looking for a more modern, urban image.

But why the hell would they want to kill a high-school boy like Michael Karnes? Why would one of these fanatics – Judge – be engaged in a campaign against promiscuous teenagers, ranting on the phone about sin and judgment? What did that have to do with making the world safe for the white race? Michael Karnes had been a white-bread boy – not a natural target for something like the Aryan Alliance but a potential recruit.

The blacktop in the parking lot was soft in places.

The summer sky was gas-flame blue. And as blind as a dead television screen, offering no answers.

Chase started the car and drove home.

No one shot at him.

In his room, he turned on the television, watched it for fifteen minutes, and turned it off because the program was finished. He opened a paperback book, but he couldn't concentrate on the story.

He paced, instinctively staying away from his window.

*   *   *

At six o'clock he left the house to keep his date with Glenda Kleaver.

To avoid leading Judge to the woman and perhaps endangering her, Chase drove aimlessly for half an hour, turning at random from street to street, watching his rearview mirror. But no tail stayed with him along his circuitous route.

Glenda lived in an inexpensive but well-kept garden-apartment complex on St. John's Circle, on the third floor of a three-floor building. There was a peephole in her door, and she took the time to use it before answering his knock. She was wearing white shorts and a dark blue blouse.

'You're punctual,' she said. 'Come in. Can I get you something to drink?'

As he stepped inside, he said, 'What're you having?'

'Iced tea. But I've got beer, wine, gin, vodka.'

'Iced tea sounds good.'

'Be right back.'

He watched her as she crossed the room and

disappeared down a short corridor that evidently led to the dining room and kitchen. She moved like sunlight on water.

The living room was sparsely furnished but cozy. Four armchairs, a coffee table, a couple of end tables with lamps. No sofa. There were no paintings because all the walls without windows were covered with bookshelves, and every shelf was crammed full of paperbacks and book-club hardbacks.

He was reading the titles on the spines of the books when she returned with two glasses of iced tea. 'You're a reader,' he said.

'I confess.'

'Me too.'

'See any shared interests?'

'Quite a few,' he said, accepting the tea. He pulled a volume off one shelf. 'What did you think of this?'

'It reeked.'

'Didn't it?'

'All the publicity, but it's empty.'

He returned the book to the shelf, and they adjourned to two of the armchairs.

'I like people,' Glenda said, which seemed an odd comment until she added, 'but I like them more in books than in real life.'

'Why's that?'

'I'm sure you know,' she said.

And he did. 'In a book, even the real bastards can't hurt you.'

'And you can never lose a friend you make in a book.'

'When you get to a sad part, no one's there to see you cry.'

'Or wonder why you don't cry when you should,' she said.

'I don't mind living secondhand. Through books.'

'It has big advantages,' she agreed.

He wondered who had hurt her, how often, and how badly. Beyond doubt, she had suffered. He could sense a depth of pain in her that was disturbingly familiar to him.

Yet there was nothing melancholy about her. She had a sweet, gentle smile, and she virtually radiated a quiet happiness that made him more comfortable in her living room than he had been anywhere since he'd left home for college seven years ago.

'When I returned to the reference desk at the morgue and you'd gone,' she said, 'I thought you were angry about being made to wait.'

'Not at all. I just remembered ... an appointment I'd forgotten.'

'I'll be back on duty Monday if you want to stop around.'

'You like working there?'

'It's nice and quiet. Some of the reporters can be too flirty, but that's the worst of it.'

He smiled. 'You can handle them.'

'Reporters all think they're persistent and tough,' she said. 'But they're no match for a newspaper-morgue librarian.'

'At least not for this one.'

'Where do you work?' she asked.

'Nowhere right now.'

'Waiting,' she said, instead of anything that anyone else might have said. 'Sometimes waiting is the hardest thing.'

'But it's all you can do.'

She sipped her iced tea. 'One day there'll be a door like any other door, but when you open it, right in front of you will be just the thing you need.'

'It's nice to think so,' he said.

'Then you forget the pain of waiting.'

Chase had never been party to a conversation half as strange as this – yet it made more sense than any conversation that he'd ever had in his life.

'Have you found that door?' he asked.

'There's not just one. A series of them. With spells of waiting in between.'

Dinner was delicious: tossed salad, potatoes and pasta layered with spinach and basil and feta cheese, zucchini with slivers of red pepper, and marinated sea bass lightly grilled. For dessert, fresh orange slices sprinkled with coconut.

When they weren't talking in that strange shorthand that came naturally to them, they fell into silences that were never awkward.

After dinner in the dining area off the kitchen, she suggested that they adjourn to the small balcony off the living room, but Chase said, 'What about the dishes?'

'I'll take care of them later.'

'I'll help, and we'll get them done twice as fast.'

'A man who offers to wash dishes.'

'I thought maybe I could *dry*.'

After the dishes, they sat on a pair of lawn chairs on the balcony in the warm July darkness. The garden courtyard was below. Voices drifted to them from other balconies, and city crickets made a sound as lonely as any made by their country cousins.

When at last it was time to leave, he said, 'Is this a magical apartment – or do you make it peaceful wherever you go?'

'You don't have to make the world peaceful,' she said. 'It is to begin with. You just have to learn not to disturb things.'

'I could stay here forever.'

'Stay if you want.'

The balcony had no lamp, only fireflies in the night beyond the railing. In such deep shadows,

Chase couldn't read her face.

He thought of dead women in a tunnel, half a world away, and the weight of guilt in his heart was immeasurable.

He found himself apologizing to Glenda for what she might have thought was a pass. 'I'm sorry. I had no right, I didn't mean –'

'I know,' she said softly.

'I don't want –'

'I know. Hush.'

They were silent for a while.

Then she said, 'Being alone can be good. It's easy to find peace alone. But sometimes ... being alone is a kind of death.'

He could add nothing more to what she'd said.

Later she said, 'I only have one bedroom, one bed. But the armchairs in the living room were all bought secondhand, here and there, and one of them is a lounger that pretty much folds into a bed.'

'Thank you,' he said.

Later still, as he sat in the lounger, reading a book from her shelves, she reappeared, dressed for bed in a T-shirt and panties. She leaned down, kissed his cheek, and said, 'Good night, Ben.'

He put down his book and took her hand in both of his. 'I'm not sure what's happening here.'

'Do you find it strange?'

'I should.'

'But?'

'I don't.'

'All that happened is – we both found the same doorway from different sides.'

'And now?'

'We give it time, enough time, and see if this is what we need,' she said.

'You're special.'

'And you're not?'

'I know I'm not,' he said.

'You're wrong.'

She kissed him again and went to bed.

And later still, after he had converted the chair into its fullest reclining position, turned off the lamp on the end table, and settled down, she returned in the darkness and sat across from him. He did not hear her coming as much as feel the serenity that she brought with her.

'Ben?' she said.

'Yes?'

'Everyone is damaged.'

'Not everyone,' he said.

'Yes. Everyone. Not just you, not just me.'

He knew why she had waited for darkness. Some things were not easily said in the light.

'I don't know if I can ever ... be with a woman again,' he said. 'The war. What happened. No one knows. I have this guilt ...'

'Of course you do. Good men wear chains of guilt all their lives. They feel.'

'This is . . . this is worse than what other men have done.'

'We learn, we change, or we die,' she said quietly.

He couldn't speak.

From the darkness, she said, 'When I was a little girl, I had to give what I never wanted to give, day after day, week after week, year after year, to a father who didn't know the meaning of guilt.'

'I'm so sorry.'

'You needn't be. That's long ago,' she said. 'Many doors away from where I am now.'

'I should never touch you.'

'Hush. You will touch me one day, and I'll be happy for your touch. Maybe next week. Next month. Maybe a year from now or even longer. Whenever you're ready. Everyone is damaged, Ben, but the heart can be repaired.'

When she rose from her chair and returned to the bedroom, she left a place of peace behind her, and Ben found a sleep without nightmares.

* * *

Sunday morning, Glenda was still sleeping soundly when Ben went to her bedroom to check on her. He stood in the doorway for a long while, listening to her slow, steady breathing, which seemed to him to have all the subtle power of a gentle tide breaking on a beach.

He left her a note in the kitchen: *I've got some business to take care of. Will call soon. Love, Ben.*

The morning sun was already fiercely hot. The sky was gas-flame blue, as it had been the previous day, but it no longer seemed like a flat, blind vault. It was a deep sky now, with places beyond.

He returned to his apartment, where he encountered Mrs. Fielding in the front hall.

'Been out all night?' she asked, eyeing the rumpled clothes in which he'd slept. 'You didn't have an accident, did you?'

'No,' he said, climbing the stairs, 'and I wasn't bar hopping the topless joints either.'

He was surprised that he had been able to be brusque with her, and she was so startled that she had no reply.

After a shower and a shave, he sat with his notebook of clues, trying to decide what his next step should be.

When the telephone rang, he hoped it was Glenda, but Judge said, 'So you've found yourself a bitch in heat, have you?'

Ben *knew* that he hadn't been followed to Glenda's apartment.

Judge could be aware of nothing more than that he'd been out all night; the bastard was just assuming that he'd been with a woman.

'Killer and fornicator,' Judge accused.

'I know what you look like,' Ben said. 'About my height, blond, with a long thin nose. You walk with your shoulders hunched. You're a neat dresser.'

Judge was amused. 'With that and the entire U.S. Army to help you search, you might find me in time, Chase.'

'You're part of the brotherhood.'

The killer was silent. This was a nervous silence and therefore different from his usual judgmental silences.

'The Aryan Alliance,' Ben said. 'You and Eric Blentz. You and a lot of other moronic assholes who think you're the master race.'

'You don't want to cross certain people, Mr. Chase.'

'You don't scare me. I've been dead for years anyway. You've got a dead man looking for you, Judge, and we dead men never stop.'

With sudden anger hotter than the July morning, Judge said, 'You don't know anything about me, Chase, not anything that matters – and you're not going to get a chance to learn anything more.'

'Whoa, easy, easy,' Ben said, enjoying being on

the delivery end of the needle for a change. 'You master-race guys, you come from a lot of inbreeding, cousins lying with cousins, sisters with brothers, makes you a little unstable sometimes.'

Judge was silent again, and when he finally spoke, he sounded as if he was shaking with the effort to control his anger. 'Do you like your new bitch, Chase? Isn't that the name of the good witch in the land of Oz? Glenda the good witch?'

Ben's heart felt as if it had turned over. He tried to fake bafflement: 'Who? What're you talking about?'

'Glenda, tall and golden.'

There was *no way* that he had been followed to her apartment.

'Works in a morgue,' said Judge.

He couldn't know.

'Dead newspapers. I think I'll send the fornicating bitch to another kind of morgue, Chase, a morgue where the dead have some real *meat* on them.'

Judge hung up.

He couldn't know.

But he did.

Suddenly Chase felt pursued by a supernatural avenger. Justice had come for him at last. Out of those faraway, long-ago tunnels.

10

Glenda answered Ben's knock, read the anxiety in his eyes, and said, 'What's wrong?'

Once inside, he closed the front door and engaged both the latch and the deadbolt.

'Ben?' She was wearing a pink T-shirt, white shorts, and tennis shoes. Her golden hair was pulled back in a pair of ponytails, one behind each ear, and even as tall as she was, she still seemed like a little girl. In spite of what she'd told him in the darkness last night, she was the personification of innocence.

'Do you own a gun?' he asked.

'No.'

'Neither do I. Didn't want to see a gun after the war. Now nothing would make me happier than to have one in my hand.'

In the dining area off the kitchen, at the table where they'd had dinner the previous night, he told her about Judge, everything since the murder of Michael Karnes. 'Now . . . because of me . . . you're part of it.'

She reached across the small table and took his hand. 'No. That's the wrong way to look at it. Now, because we met, we're in it together – and you're no longer alone.'

'I want to call Detective Wallace, ask him to provide you with protection.'

'Why should he believe you any more now than he did before?' she asked.

'The damage to my car, when the guy sideswiped it out at the mall, trying to run me down.'

'He won't believe that's how it happened. You don't have any witnesses. He'll say you were drinking.'

Ben knew that she was right. 'We need to get help *somewhere.*'

'You were handling it on your own, tracking him down on your own. So why not the two of us now?'

He shook his head. 'That was all right when it was only my life on the line. But now – '

'People in books,' she said.

'What?'

'We can trust people in books. But here, right now – we can't trust anyone but ourselves.'

He was scared as he had not been in a long time. Not scared only for her. Scared for himself. Because at last he had something to lose.

'But how do we find the creep?' he wondered.

'We do whatever you were going to do on your own. First, call Louise Allenby. Find out if she got the name of the guy who dated her mother, the guy with the Aryan Alliance ring.'

'He won't be Judge. Louise would have recognized him.'

'But he might be a link to Judge.'

'That would be too neat.'

'Sometimes life *is* neat.'

Ben called the Allenby house, and Louise answered. When she heard who it was, her voice dropped into a seductive purr. She had the name he wanted, but she wouldn't give it to him on the telephone.

'You'll have to come around and see me,' she said coquettishly. 'My mom's away for the weekend with this guy. Got the place all to myself.'

* * *

When Louise answered the bell, she was wearing a yellow bikini, and she smelled of coconut tanning lotion. Opening the door, she said, 'I knew you'd be back to get the reward –'

When she saw Glenda, she fell silent.

'May we come in?' Ben asked.

Louise stepped back, confused, and closed the door behind them.

169

Ben introduced Glenda as a close friend, and Louise's face soured into a pout.

Heading to the living room, rolling her hips to show off her tight butt, the girl said, 'Will you have a drink this time?'

'Early, isn't it?'

'Noon.'

'No, thanks,' Ben said. 'We've only got a couple of questions, and we'll be going.'

At the wet bar, Louise stood with her right hip cocked, mixing her drink.

Ben and Glenda sat on the sofa, and Louise carried her drink to an armchair opposite them. The girl slouched in the chair, with her legs spread. The crotch of her skimpy swimsuit conformed to the folds of flesh that it was supposed to conceal, leaving nothing to the imagination.

Chase felt uncomfortable, but Glenda seemed as serene as ever.

'The name you wanted,' Louise said, 'is Tom Deekin. The guy who dated my mom, the guy with the ring. He sells insurance. Has an office over on Canby Street by the firehouse. But he isn't the guy who knifed Mike.'

'I know. Still . . . he might be able to give us the names of other people in the brotherhood.'

'Fat chance.' She was holding her drink in one hand and lightly caressing one well-tanned thigh with the other, trying to make her self-appreciation seem unconscious but being too blatant by half. 'These guys are committed to something, you know, they have ideals – and you're an outsider. Why're they going to tell you anything?'

'They might.'

She smiled and shook her head. 'You think maybe you can squeeze a few names out of Tom Deekin? Listen, these guys have steel balls. They have to be tough, getting ready to defend against the nappy-heads and the kikes and the rest of them.'

Ben supposed that some members of the Aryan Alliance might be dangerous – but most of them were probably playing at this master-race stuff, drinking beer and gassing about racial Armageddon instead of watching football games on the tube.

Glenda said, 'Louise, as I understand it, you'd gone with Mike for a year before . . .'

'Before that fruitcake gutted him?' Louise said, as if to prove that she was as tough as anyone. Or maybe the coldness in her was as real as it seemed. 'A year – yeah, that's about right. Why?'

'Did you ever notice anyone following you – as if they were keeping a watch on you?'

'No.'

Ben knew what Glenda was after. Judge researched his potential victims to discover their sins, to attempt to justify his murderous urges as righteous judgments. He had followed Mike and Louise; he'd told Ben as much; therefore, they might have noticed him.

'You answered too fast, without thinking,' Ben said. 'Glenda doesn't mean was someone following you recently. Maybe it was even weeks ago, even months ago.'

Louise hesitated, sipping her drink. Her free hand slid from her thigh to the crotch of her bikini. Her fingertips moved in slow circles over the yellow fabric.

Though she stared mostly at Ben, the girl occasionally glanced assessingly at Glenda. She clearly felt that they were engaged in a competition.

Glenda, in her serenity, had won all the necessary races years ago – and had never run against anyone but herself.

Louise said, 'The beginning of the year, about February and March, there was something like that. Some creep hanging around – but it never amounted to anything. It turned out not to be any mysterious stranger.'

'Not a stranger? Then who?'

'Well, when Mike first said he was following us, I just laughed, you know? Mike was like that, always off on one fantasy or another. He was going to be an artist, did you know? First he was going to work in a garret and become world famous. Jesus. Then he was going to be a paper-back-book illustrator. Then a film director, paint with the camera. He never could decide – but he knew whatever it was he would be famous and rich. A dreamer.'

'And he thought someone was watching you together?' Ben asked.

'It was this guy in a Volkswagen. A red Volks-wagen. After a week or so I saw it wasn't another fantasy. There really was this guy in the VW.'

'What did he look like?' Ben asked.

'I never saw him. He stayed far enough away. But he wasn't dangerous. Mike knew him.'

Ben felt as if the top of his head were coming off, and he wanted to shake the rest of the story out of her without having to go through this question-and-answer routine. Calmly he said, 'Who was the guy?'

'I don't know,' she said. 'Mike wouldn't tell me.'

'And you weren't curious?' he asked.

'Sure I was. But when Mike made up his mind about something, he wouldn't change it. One night, when we went to the Diamond Dell – that's a drive-in hamburger joint on Galasio – he got out of the car and went back and talked to the guy in the VW. When we came back, he said he knew him and that he wouldn't have any more trouble with him. And he was right. The guy drove away, and he didn't follow us any more. I never knew what it was about, and I forgot about it till you asked.'

'But you must have had some idea,' Ben insisted. 'You can't have let it drop without having found out something more concrete.'

She put down her drink. 'Mike didn't want to talk about it, and I thought I knew why. He never said directly, but I think maybe the weasel in the VW made a pass at him once.'

'A pass?' Ben said.

'I only think so,' she said. 'Couldn't prove it. Anyway, it couldn't be the same guy that killed him, the guy with the ring.'

'Why not?' Glenda asked.

'These Aryan Alliance guys, they hate fags every bit as much as they hate all the coloreds. No way they're ever going to let some pansy-ass wear the ring.'

'One more thing,' Ben said. 'I'd really like a list of Mike's friends, five or six guys his own age that he was close to. Someone he might have told about this guy in the red Volkswagen.'

'Five or six – you're wasting your time. Mike wasn't close to very many people. Fact is, Marty Cable was his one best friend.'

'Then we'll need to talk to Cable.'

'He's probably at Hanover Park. Summers, he works as a lifeguard at the municipal pool.' She looked more directly at Glenda than she had since they'd entered the house. 'You think Ben here is ever going to screw me?'

'Probably not,' Glenda said, evincing no surprise whatsoever at the question.

'Am I a package or not?' Louise asked.

Glenda said, 'You're a package, all right.'

'Then he must be nuts.'

'Oh, he's okay,' Glenda said.

'You think so?' the girl asked.

'Yeah,' Glenda said. 'He's a good guy.'

'If you say so, then he must be.'

The two women smiled at each other.

Then Louise took her hand from her crotch, looked at Ben, and sighed. 'Too bad.'

In the car, driving away from the house, Ben said, 'Is the world going to hell or what?'

'You mean Louise?'

'Are girls like that now?'

'Some. But there have always been some like her. She's nothing new. She's just a child.'

'She's almost eighteen, going to college in the fall, old enough to have some sense.'

'No, that's not what I mean. She's *just* a child, and she always will be. Perpetually immature, always needing to be the center of attention. Don't waste your time disliking her, Ben. What she needs is sympathy, and lots of it, because she's going to have a bad life, a load of pain.

When her looks eventually start to go, she won't know what to be.'

'She liked you, even if she didn't want to,' he said.

'A little, yeah.'

'You liked her?'

'No. But we're all God's children, right? None of us deserve what life's going to dish out to her.'

They drove along a street lined with enormous trees. Sunlight and shadow flickered across the windshield. Light and shadow. Hope and despair. Yesterday and tomorrow. Flickering.

After a while, he said, 'She's a perpetual child, but you've been grown up forever.'

'In spite of everything,' she said, 'I'm the lucky one.'

* * *

Under the trees in Hanover Park, every patch of shade had been claimed by families with picnic hampers. Sunbathers lounged on big beach towels on the lawns, and games of volleyball were under way.

The Olympic-size municipal pool was full of screaming, splashing children. A lifeguard was posted at each end, on a raised chair, and half a dozen admiring teenage girls were gathered at each station, hoping to be noticed.

Ben led Glenda through the flesh market and introduced himself to Martin Cable.

The lifeguard was lean and muscular. He had a lot of long dark hair, but his face was as beardless as that of a much younger boy.

'Sure, me and Mike were buddies,' he said when Ben asked him about Karnes. 'What's it to you?'

'I don't think the cops are doing enough to nail the killer, and I don't like the idea of some lunatic running around with a grudge against me.'

'Why should I care?'

'Your friend was killed.'

'Everybody dies. Don't you watch the evening news?'

Because Cable was wearing mirror sunglasses, Ben couldn't see the teenager's eyes. He found it unnerving to watch his twin reflections in those silvered lenses and be unable to tell for sure whether Cable's attention was focused on him, on the parade of girls, or on the swimmers in the pool.

'I wasn't there when it happened,' Cable said, 'so how could I know anything that would help?'

Glenda said, 'Don't you want Mike's killer to be caught?'

Because Cable didn't move a fraction of an inch or even tilt his head one degree to answer her, it was obvious that behind his mirror glasses, his attention was already on Glenda. 'Whatever happens,' he said cryptically.

'We talked to Louise Allenby,' Chase said.

'Entertaining, huh?'

'You know her?'

'Pretty much.'

'She said maybe Mike had some trouble with a guy a while ago.'

Cable didn't reply.

Ben said, 'She thinks this guy made a pass at him.'

Cable frowned. 'Mike, he was your fundamental pussy hound.'

'I don't doubt that.'

'Man, he didn't even get laid till he was halfway through his junior year, and then once it happened, he just went nuts for it. Couldn't keep his mind on anything else.'

Ben looked around uneasily at the teenage girls vying for the lifeguard's attention. Some were as young as fourteen or fifteen. He wanted to tell Cable to watch his language – but that would mean the end of their conversation.

'You know his parents,' Cable said, 'you can see why Mike would go off the deep end over something – pussy, drugs, booze, something just to prove he was alive.'

'I've never met his folks,' Ben said.

'Ma and Pa Tightass. He just sort of broke

loose, all at once. After that, his grades dropped. He wanted to get into State, but he wasn't going to make it if he didn't pull up his grade-point average. No college deferral. Hello, Vietnam.'

Screams rose from the pool. They could have been the shrieks of a hyperkinetic child at play or the frantic cries of a drowner. Marty Cable didn't turn to see which. He still seemed to be focused on Glenda.

'Physics was his worst subject. He had to get a tutor Saturday. The guy was a sleaze.'

'This was who made a pass at him?' Glenda asked. 'The tutor?'

'Tried to convince Mike there was nothing wrong with swinging both ways. Mike got another tutor, but this guy kept calling him.'

'You remember the name?'

'No.'

'Not even the first name?'

'No. Mike, he got another tutor, passed physics. But you stop and think about it, what was all the trouble for? He's never going to go to State after all, is he? He might've been better off just forgetting about physics and screwing his brains out. Better use of what time he had left.'

'With that attitude, then what's the point of doing *anything?*' Glenda asked.

'Is no point,' Cable said, as if he thought she was agreeing with him. 'We're all meat.' To

Chase, he said, 'You know how things really are – you were in Nam,' as if he himself understood the horrors of the war thanks to his monthly subscription to *Rolling Stone*. 'Hey, you know how many nuclear bombs the Russians have aimed at us?'

'A lot,' Chase said, impatient with the boy's cynicism.

'Twenty thousand,' Cable said. 'Enough to kill every one of us five times over.'

'I'm not too worried until it's six times.'

'Cool,' Cable said with a small laugh, impervious to sarcasm. 'Me neither. Not worried about a damn thing. Take what you can get and hope you wake up in the morning – that's the smart way to look at it.'

As a pair of squabbling crows flew low overhead, the lifeguard tilted his face toward the sky. The sun was a ferocious white fire on his mirror glasses.

* * *

Lora Karnes apparently didn't believe in makeup. Her hair was cut short and carelessly combed. Even in the July heat, she wore loose khaki slacks and a long-sleeve blouse. Although she must have been in her early forties, she seemed at least fifteen years older. She perched on the edge of her chair with her knees together, her hands folded in her lap, hunched forward like a gargoyle that was queerly disturbing yet insufficiently grotesque to be used on a cathedral parapet.

The house was as drab and quiet as the woman. The living-room furniture was heavy and dark. The drapes were shut against the July glare, and two lamps shed a peculiar gray light. On the television, an evangelist was gesticulating furiously, but the sound was muted, so he seemed like a crazed and poorly trained mime.

Framed and hung on the walls were needlepoint samplers with quotations from the Bible. Mrs. Karnes evidently had made them herself. Curiously, the quotations were obscure and enigmatic, perhaps taken out of context. Ben couldn't make much sense of them or quite grasp what spiritual guidance they were supposed to offer:

I WILL LAY MINE HAND
UPON MY MOUTH
– Job, xl, 4

PUT THEM IN MIND . . .
TO OBEY MAGISTRATES
– Titus, iii, 1

BLESSED IS HE,
WHOSOEVER SHALL NOT BE
OFFENDED IN ME
— *Luke, vii, 23*

AND JACOB SOD POTTAGE
— *Genesis, xxv, 29*

The walls also featured framed portraits of religious leaders, but the gallery was an eclectic mix: the pope, Oral Roberts, Billy Graham, a couple of faces that Chase recognized as those of tackier television evangelists with more interest in contributions than in salvation. There seemed to be a wealth of religious feeling in the Karnes house — but no clear-cut faith.

Harry Karnes was as drab as his wife and the room: short, only perhaps ten years older than Lora but so thin and prematurely aged as to be on the verge of frailty. His hands shook when they were not resting on the arms of his Barca-lounger. He could not look directly at Ben but gazed over his head when speaking to him.

On the sofa beside Glenda, Ben figured that visitors to the Karnes house were rare indeed. One day, someone would realize they hadn't heard from Lora or Harry in a while and, upon investi-gation, would find the couple sitting as they were now, but shriveled and shrunken and long mummified, dead a decade before anyone noticed.

'He was a good boy,' said Harry Karnes.

'Let's not lie to Mr. Chase,' Lora admonished.

'He did well in school, and he was going to college too,' Harry said.

'Now, Dad, we know that isn't truthful,' Lora said. 'He went wild.'

'Later, yes. But before that, Mother, he was a good boy,' said Harry.

'He went wild, and you'd not have thought he was the same boy from one year to the next. Running around. Always out later than he should be. How could it end any way but what it did?'

The longer that Chase remained in the warm, stuffy house, the chillier he became. 'I'm particularly interested in this physics tutor he had back in the beginning of the year.'

Lora Karnes frowned. 'Like I said, the second teacher's name was Bandoff, but I don't remember the first. Do you, Dad?'

'It's in the back of my mind, Mother, but I can't quite see it,' said Harry Karnes, and he turned his attention to the silently ranting preacher on the television.

'Didn't you have to pay the man?' Glenda asked.

'Well, but it was in cash. Never wrote out a check,' said Lora Karnes. She glanced disapprovingly at Glenda's bare legs, then looked quickly away, as though embarrassed. 'Besides, he only tutored for a couple of weeks. Michael couldn't learn from him, and we had to get Mr. Bandoff.'

'How did you find the first tutor?'

'Michael found him through the school. Both were through the school.'

'The high school where Mike attended classes?'

'Yes, but this teacher didn't work there. He taught at George Washington High, on the other side of town, but he was on the list of recommended tutors.'

'Michael was a smart boy,' Harry said.

'Smart is never smart enough,' his wife said.

'He could have been something someday.'

'Not with just being smart,' his wife corrected.

The Karneses made Ben nervous. He couldn't figure them out. They were fanatics of some sort, but they seemed to have gone down their own strange little trail in the wilderness of disorganized – as opposed to organized – religion.

'If he hadn't gone wild like he did,' Lora said, 'he might've made something of himself. But he couldn't control himself. And then how could it end any way but how it did?'

Glenda said, 'Do you remember anything at all about the first tutor – where he lived? Didn't Mike go there for the lessons?'

'Yes,' said Lora Karnes. 'I think it was in that nice little neighborhood over on the west side, with all the bungalows.'

'Crescent Heights?' Glenda suggested.

'That's it.'

Turning away from the television, looking over his wife's head, Harry said, 'Mother, wasn't the fella's name Lupinski, Lepenski – something like that?'

'Dad, you're right. That was his name. Linski.'

'Richard?' Harry suggested

'Exactly, Dad. Richard Linski.'

'But he wasn't any good,' Harry told the wall past Ben's left shoulder. 'So we got the second tutor, and then Michael's grades improved. He was a good boy.'

'Once, he was, Dad. And you know, I don't blame him for it all. Plenty of blame for us to share in it.'

Ben felt their weird gloom sucking him down as surely as if he'd been caught in a whirlpool in a dark sea.

Glenda said, 'Can you spell that last name for me.'

'L-i-n-s-k-i,' said Lora.

Richard Linski.

'Michael didn't like him,' Lora said.

'Michael was a good boy, Mother.' Harry had tears in his eyes.

Seeing her husband's condition, Lora Karnes said, 'Let's not blame the boy too much, Dad. I agree. He wasn't wicked.'

'Can't blame a child for all its faults, Mother.'

'You have to go back to the parents, Dad. If Michael wasn't so perfect, then it's because we weren't perfect ourselves.'

As if speaking to the muted evangelist on the television, Harry Karnes said, 'You can't raise a godly child when you've done wicked things yourself.'

Afraid that the couple was about to descend into a series of teary confessions that would make no more sense than the words on the needlepoint samplers, Ben abruptly got to his feet and took Glenda's hand as she rose beside him. 'Sorry to have brought this all back into your minds again.'

'Not at all,' Lora Karnes said. 'Memory chastens.'

One of the quotations on the walls caught Ben's eye:

SEVEN THUNDERS UTTERED THEIR VOICES

– Revelation, x, 3.

'Mrs Karnes,' Ben said, 'did you make the samplers yourself?'

'Yes. Needlepoint helps keep my hands to the Lord's work.'

'They're lovely. But I was wondering ... what does that one mean exactly?'

'Seven thunders all at once,' she said quietly, without fervor – in fact, with an unnervingly calm authority that made it seem as if what she said must surely make sense. 'That's how it will be. And then we'll know why we've always got to do our best. Then we'll wish we'd done better, much better, when the seven thunders roll all at once.'

At the front door, as Ben and Glenda were leaving, Mrs. Karnes said, 'Does God work through you, Mr. Chase?'

'Doesn't He work through all of us?' Ben asked.

'No. Some aren't strong enough. But you – are you His hand, Mr. Chase?'

He had no idea what answer she wanted. 'I don't think so, Mrs. Karnes.'

She followed them onto the front walk. 'I think you are.'

'Then God works in even more mysterious ways than anyone ever knew before.'

'I think you are God's hand.'

The scorching, late-afternoon sun was oppressive, but Lora Karnes still chilled Ben. He turned from her without another word.

The woman was still standing in the doorway, watching, as they drove away in the battered Mustang.

* * *

All day, from Glenda's apartment to the Allenby house to Hanover Park to the Karneses' house, Ben had driven evasively, and both he and Glenda had looked for a tail. No one had followed them at any point in their rambling journey.

No one followed them from the Karneses' house either. They drove until they found a service station with a pay phone.

On the floor of the booth, an army of ants was busy moving the carcass of a dead beetle.

Glenda stood at the open door while Ben searched for Richard Linski in the directory. He found a number. In Crescent Heights.

With change from Glenda's purse, Ben made the call.

It rang twice. Then: 'Hello?'

Ben said nothing,

'Hello?' Richard Linski said. 'Is anyone there?'

Quietly, Ben hung up.

'Well?' Glenda asked.

'It's him. Judge's real name is Richard Linski.'

11

The motel room was small, filled with the rumble of the window-mounted air-conditioner.

Ben closed the door and checked the dead-bolt to be sure that it worked properly. He tested the security chain; it was well fitted.

'You're safe enough if you stay here,' he said. 'Linski can't know where you are.'

To avoid giving Judge a chance to find them, they hadn't gone back to her apartment to pack a bag for her. They had checked in without luggage. If everything went well, they wouldn't be staying the whole night anyway. This was just a way station between the loneliness of the past and whatever future fate might grant them.

Sitting on the edge of the bed, still childlike in her pink socks and twin ponytails, she said, 'I should go with you.'

'I have combat training. You don't. It's that simple.'

She didn't ask him why he hadn't called the police. With what they had learned, even Detective Wallace would at least question Linski – and if Linski was the killer, then the evidence would fall into place. Anyone else would have asked him that tough question – but she was not like anyone else.

Night had fallen.

'I better go,' he said.

She got off the edge of the bed and came into his arms. For a while he held her.

By unspoken mutual consent, they didn't kiss. A kiss would have been a promise. In spite of his combat training, however, he might not leave Linski's house alive. He didn't want to make a promise to her that he might be unable to fulfill.

He unlocked the door, took the chain off, and stepped outside onto the concrete promenade. He waited for her to close the door and engage the deadbolt.

The night was warm and humid. The sky was bottomless.

He left the motel in his Mustang.

* * *

At ten o'clock, Ben parked two blocks from Richard Linski's house and put on a pair of gardening gloves that he had purchased earlier. He made the rest of the journey on foot, staying on the opposite side of the street from the house.

The well-kept house was the second from the corner: white brick with emerald-green trim and dark-green slate roof. It was set on two well-landscaped lots, and the entire property was ringed with waist-high hedges that were so even they might have been trimmed with the aid of a quality micrometer.

Some windows glowed. Linski was apparently at home.

Ben walked the street that ran perpendicular to the one on which the bungalow faced. He entered a narrow, deserted alleyway that led behind the property.

A wrought-iron gate punctuated the wall of hedges. It wasn't locked. He opened it and went into Linski's backyard.

The rear porch was not so deep as the one at the front. It was bracketed by large lilac bushes. The boards didn't creak under his feet.

Lights were on in the kitchen, filtered through red-and-white-checkered curtains.

He waited a few minutes in the lilac-scented darkness, not thinking about anything, geared down and idling, preparing himself for confrontation as he had learned to do in Nam.

The back door was locked when he quietly tried it. But both kitchen windows were open to admit the night breeze.

Deeper in the house, a radio was playing big-band music. Benny Goodman. *One O'clock Jump.*

Stooping low, he brought his face to the window and peered between the half-drawn curtains, which stirred in the gentle breeze. He saw a pine table and chairs, a straw basket full of apples in the center of the table, a refrigerator, and double ovens. Cannisters for flour and sugar and coffee. A utensil rack holding scoops and ladles and big spoons and cooking forks. A blender plugged into a wall outlet.

No Judge. Linski was elsewhere in the house. Glenn Miller. *String of Pearls.*

Ben examined the window screen and found that it was held in place by simple pressure clips. He removed the screen and set it aside.

The table was just beyond the window. He had to climb onto it as he went inside, careful not to knock over the basket of apples. From the table he eased himself silently to the vinyl-tile floor.

The music on the radio covered what small noises he made.

Acutely aware that he was without a weapon, he considered trying the drawers in the cupboard by the sink and securing a sharp knife, but he quickly dismissed that idea. A knife would bring events to an unnerving point, full circle, except that now he himself would be the slasher – and would be forced to confront directly the issue of not Linski's sanity but his own.

He paused at the archway between the kitchen and the dining room, because there were no lights in that intervening space except what spilled into it from the kitchen and living room. He didn't dare risk stumbling over anything in the dark.

When his eyes adjusted to the shadows, he edged across the room. Here, a deep-pile carpet absorbed his footsteps.

He stood at the threshold of the front room, letting his eyes adjust to the brighter light.

Someone coughed. A man.

In Nam, when a mission was especially tense, Ben had been able to devote his mind to its completion with a singleness of purpose that he had never achieved before or since. He wanted to be as brisk and clean and quick about this as he had been about those wartime operations, but he was bothered by thoughts of Glenda waiting alone and surely wondering if the motel-room door would be one of those *special* doors beyond which lay the thing that she needed.

He flexed his gloved hands and drew a slow breath. Preparing himself.

The smart thing to do was to turn around right now, cross the darkened dining room as quietly as possible, cross the kitchen, leave by the back door, and call the police.

But they would be real police. Not like the

police in books. Perhaps reliable. Perhaps not.

He stepped into the living room.

In a large armchair near the fireplace sat a man with an open newspaper on his lap. He wore tortoiseshell reading glasses pushed far down on his thin, straight nose, and he was humming along with Glenn Miller's tune while reading the comics.

Briefly, Ben thought that he had made a grave mistake, because he couldn't quite believe that a psychotic killer, like anyone else, could become happily engrossed in the latest exploits of Snoopy and Charlie Brown and Broom Hilda. Then the man looked up, surprised, and he fit Judge's description: tall, blond, ascetic.

'Richard Linski?' Ben asked.

The man in the chair seemed frozen in place, perhaps a mannequin propped there to distract Ben while the real Judge, the real Richard Linski, crept up on him from behind. The illusion was so complete that Ben almost turned to see if his fear was warranted.

'*You*,' Linski whispered.

He wadded the comic pages in his hands and threw them aside as he exploded out of the armchair.

All fear left Ben, and he was unnaturally calm.

'What are *you* doing here?' Linski asked, and his voice was without doubt the voice of Judge.

He backed away from the chair, toward the fireplace. His hands were feeling behind him for something. The fireplace poker.

'Don't try it,' Chase said.

Instead of making a grab for the brass poker, Linski snatched something off the mantel, from beside an ormolu clock: a silencer-fitted pistol.

The clock had hidden it.

Ben stepped forward as Linski brought the weapon up, but he did not move quite fast enough. The bullet took him in the left shoulder and twisted him sideways, off balance, and into the floor lamp.

He fell, taking the lamp with him. Both bulbs smashed when they struck the floor, plunging the room into near-total darkness that was relieved only by the weak light from distant streetlamps outside and the faint glow from the kitchen.

'Fornicator,' Judge whispered.

Ben's shoulder felt as if a nail had been driven into it, and his arm was half numb. He lay still, playing dead in the dark.

'Chase?'

Ben waited.

Linski stepped away from the mantel, bent forward as he tried to make out Ben's body in the jumble of shadows and furniture. Ben couldn't be certain, but he thought the killer was holding the pistol straight out in front of him, like a teacher holding a pointer toward a chalkboard.

'Chase?'

Weak, trembling, cold, sweating, Ben knew that shock accounted for his sudden weakness more than the wound did. He could overcome shock.

'How's our hero now?' Judge asked.

Chase launched himself at Linski, ignoring the flash of pain in his shoulder.

The pistol fired – the *whoosh* of the silencer was clearly audible in such close quarters – but Ben was under the weapon by then, and the round passed over him, shattering glass at the other end of the room.

He dragged Linski down, past the fireplace, into the television which toppled off its stand. It struck the wall and then the floor with two solid thumps, though the screen did not shatter.

The pistol flew from Linski's hand and clattered into the gloom.

Ben bore Linski all the way down onto the floor and drove his knee into his crotch.

With a dry and nearly silent scream of pain, Linski tried to throw Ben off, but he couldn't manage more than a weak shudder of protest.

Ben's wounded shoulder seemed afire. In spite of the pain, he throttled Linski with both hands, unerringly finding the right pressure points with his thumbs, as he'd been trained, applying as little pressure as possible but enough to put Linski out.

Getting to his feet, swaying like a drunk, Ben fumbled in the darkness until he found a lamp that hadn't been knocked over.

Linski was on the floor, unconscious, his arms out like wings at his sides, as if he were a bird that had fallen from the sky and broken its back on a thrust of rock.

Ben wiped his face with one gloved hand. His stomach, knotted with fear, now loosened too quickly, and he felt as if he might be sick.

Outside, a car full of shouting teenagers went by, screeched at the corner, sounded its horn, and peeled off with a squeal of rubber.

Ben stepped across Richard Linski and looked out the window. There was no one in sight. The lawn was dark. The sounds of the struggle had not carried any distance.

He turned from the window and listened to Linski's breathing. Shallow but steady.

A quick examination of his shoulder indicated that the bullet probably had passed straight through. He wasn't bleeding much, but he'd have to take a closer look at the wound as soon as possible.

In the half bath off the kitchen, he found two rolls of first-aid adhesive tape, enough to securely bind Linski. He dragged the killer into the kitchen and bound him to one of the breakfast chairs.

In the master bathroom, Chase took off his gloves and set them aside to avoid getting them bloody. He stripped out of his blood-soaked shirt and dropped it into the sink.

He took a bottle of rubbing alcohol from the medicine cabinet. When he poured it into the wound, he nearly passed out in agony. For a while he bent over the sink, paralyzed by the pain.

When he could move again, he packed the wound with wads of paper towels until the bleeding slowed even further. He slapped a wash cloth over the wound and then wound wide adhesive tape over the entire mess. It wasn't a professional bandage, but it would ensure that he didn't get blood over everything.

In the bedroom, he took one of Linski's shirts from the closet and struggled into it. He was stiffening fast from the wound.

In the kitchen again, he found a box of large plastic garbage bags and brought one to the master bathroom. He dropped his bloody shirt into it. He used paper towels to wipe his blood off the sink and the mirror, and threw those in the garbage bag when he was done. Standing in the doorway, pulling on his gardening gloves, he studied the bathroom, decided that there was no trace of what he had done, turned off the light, and closed the door.

On his way downstairs, he stumbled and had to grab the railing for support. A spell of vertigo pulled a spinning darkness into the edges of his vision – but then it passed.

Judge's second shot had missed Chase, but it had thoroughly smashed a three-foot-square ornamental mirror that had hung on the wall above the bar at the far end of the living room. All the glass had fallen out of the ornate bronze frame, and fragments were scattered over a six-foot radius. In five minutes he had picked up all the major shards, but hundreds of slivers still sparkled in the nap of the carpet and in the upholstery of nearby chairs.

He was considering this problem when Richard Linski awoke and called out.

Ben went to the chair in the kitchen. Linski's wrists were taped to the arms, each ankle to a chair leg. He twisted and tried to break free, but stopped when he realized that he wouldn't be able to pull loose.

Ben said, 'Where is your vacuum sweeper?'

'What?' Linski was still groggy.

'Vacuum.'

'What do you want that for?'

Ben threatened to backhand him.

'In the cellarway,' Linski said.

Ben took the vacuum to the living room and swept up every piece of shattered mirror that caught his attention. Fifteen minutes later, satisfied with the job that he'd done, he put the sweeper away again, just as he had found it.

He secreted the damaged mirror frame in a corner of the garage, behind a stack of other junk.

'What are you doing?' Judge asked.

Ben didn't answer him.

In the living room again, he replaced the television on its stand, plugged it in, switched it on. A situation comedy was playing, one of those in which the father is always an idiot and the mother is little better. The kids are cute monsters.

Afraid that his spells of dizziness were soon going to progress to disorientation, Ben righted the overturned floor lamp and examined the metal shade. It was dented, but there was no way to tell that the dent was new. He unscrewed the damaged lightbulbs; along with the larger scraps of the broken mirror, he threw them into the plastic garbage bag on top of the bloody shirt and paper towels. He used the pages of a magazine to scoop up the smaller pieces, and threw those and the magazine into the garbage bag.

Returning to the kitchen, Ben said, 'Where do

you keep spare lightbulbs?'

'Go to hell.'

Ben noticed that there were no red marks on the skin over Linski's carotid arteries. The pressure had been pinpoint and too briefly applied to produce bruises.

Without Linski's help, Ben required almost five minutes to find the spare lightbulbs in the back of a kitchen cabinet. He screwed two new 60-watt bulbs into the living-room lamp. The lamp lit when he switched it on.

In the kitchen again, he got a bucket of water, soap, ammoniated cleanser, and – from the refrigerator – a carton of milk, his mother's favorite spot remover. Back in the living room, with several rags and a sponge, he worked on the few small smears of his blood that marred the carpet. When he was done, the faint stubborn stains that remained were all but invisible in the long dark-brown nap. The room wouldn't have to pass a full forensic investigation, anyway. As long as it appeared that nothing had happened there, the police wouldn't take a closer look.

He put the cleaning materials away. He threw the rags into the garbage bag with the other items.

After that, he stood in the center of the room and slowly searched it for traces of the fight. The only thing that might draw anyone's suspicion was the pale, soot-ringed square where the ornate mirror had hung.

Ben pulled the two picture hangers out of the wall; they left small nail holes behind. He used a handful of paper towels to wipe away most of the dirty ring, successfully feathering the dirt to blend the lighter and darker portions of the wall. It was still obvious that something had hung there, though one might now think that it had been removed several months ago.

After locating the pistol that had flown out of Linski's hand, Ben returned to the kitchen. 'I have some questions to ask you.'

'Fuck you,' Linski said.

Ben put the muzzle of the pistol against the bridge of his captive's nose.

Linski stared. Then: 'You wouldn't.'

'Remember my war record.'

Linski paled but still glared at him.

'The silencer's homemade. Is this something the average physics teacher does for a hobby?'

'It's part of what we learn in the Alliance. Survival skills.'

'Real Boy Scouts, huh?'

'It may be funny to you, but someday you'll be glad we taught ourselves good defense. Guns, explosives, lock-picking – everything we'll need for the day when the cities burn and we have to fight for our race.'

'What does the Aryan Alliance have to do with this, anyway?'

Linski's manner changed. He grew less arrogant and nervously licked his lips.

'I've got to understand what's going on. I have to know if they're going to come after me,' Ben said, 'this whole crazy group. And if they are – why? What did I step into the middle of when I pulled you out of that car on lovers' lane?'

When Linski didn't reply, Ben put the muzzle of the pistol against his right eye, so he could look directly into the barrel.

Linski sagged in the chair. A sudden despair seized him. 'It goes back a way.'

'What does?'

'The Aryan Alliance.'

'Tell me.'

'We were in our twenties then.'

'We?'

'Lora, Harry. Me.'

'Karnes? His parents?'

'That's how we met. Through the Alliance.'

The connection so surprised Ben that he wondered if he were hallucinating the conversation. The pain in his shoulder had spread to his neck and up the back of his skull.

'They fell on hard times. Harry out of work. Lora was ill. But they had . . . the boy.'

'Mike.'

'He was a beautiful child.'

Ben knew, didn't want to hear, had no choice but to listen.

'An exquisitely beautiful child,' said Linski, clearly seeing the boy in his mind's eye. 'Three, almost four years old.'

Ben no longer pressed the pistol to Linski's eye. Now that he had started, the killer would need no encouragement to continue. His entire demeanor had changed – and he almost seemed relieved to be forced to this confession. He was unburdening himself for his own sake more than Ben's.

'I had some money, a trust fund, Lora and Harry needed money . . . and I needed what they had.'

'They sold him to you.'

'They set a high price for a night now and then,' Linski said.

'His own parents,' Ben said, remembering Lora and Harry Karnes and the enigmatic needlepoint quotations on their living-room walls.

'A high price in more ways than one.'

'How long did that go on?' Ben asked.

'Less than a year. Then . . . remorse, you know.'

'You realized it was wrong?'

'Them.' Linski's voice, gray with despair, was briefly enlivened by sarcasm: 'They had the money they needed, they were out of their financial trouble . . . so they were in a better position to find their misplaced scruples. They denied me the boy and told me to stay away forever. He was such a little angel. Forever, they said. It was so difficult. They threatened to tell others in the Alliance that I'd molested Mikey without their knowledge. There are some members who would take me out in the woods and shoot me in the back of the head if they knew what I am. I couldn't risk exposure.'

'And all these years . . .'

'I watched Mikey from a distance,' Linski said. 'Watched him as he grew up. He was never again as beautiful as when he'd been so young, so innocent. But I was growing older and *hated* growing older. Year by year, I became more aware that I'd never have . . . never have anyone . . . anything as beautiful as Mikey again. He was always there to remind me of the best time of my life, the brief best time of my life.'

'How did you manage to get the tutoring job? Why would he come to you of all people?'

'He didn't remember me.'

'You're sure?'

'Yes. That was a terrible realization . . . knowing that every kindness I'd shown him was forgotten . . . every tenderness forgotten. I think he forgot not just me but *everything* that happened . . . being touched, being adored . . . when he was four.'

Ben didn't know if his worsening nausea was

a result of his wound or of Linski's strange characterization of the molestation.

The killer sighed with regret. 'What do any of us remember from that far back? Time steals everything from us. Anyway, when he needed a tutor, he came to me because I was on the list the school gave him. Maybe it was a subconscious recollection of my name that made him choose me. I'd like to think he still held *some* memory of me even if he wasn't aware of it. However, I think it was really just pure chance. Fate.'

'So you told him what you'd done to him when he was little?'

'No. No, no. But I tried ... to reawaken his desire.'

'It was focused on girls by then.'

'He shunned me,' Linski said, not with anger, not in a cold mad voice, but with deep sadness. 'And then he told his parents, and they threatened me again. My hope was raised, you see ... raised and then shattered forever. It was so unfair to have it raised and then ... nothing. It hurt.'

'Lora and Harry ... they must have suspected you killed him.'

'Who're they to point a finger?' Linski said.

'They gave me your name.'

Ben thought of the way in which they had directed him toward Linski: Harry pretending to recall the tutor's name only with effort, getting it only half right, and Lora correcting him. Too gutless to violate the sixth commandment and seek the vengeance they wanted, they had contrived to see in Ben the hand of God and had deviously pointed him toward this man.

'I should have passed judgement on Harry and Lora too,' Linski said but without anger. 'For letting the boy become what he became.'

'It had nothing to do with what the boy had become. You killed him because you couldn't have him.'

In a still, solemn voice, Linski said, 'No. That isn't it at all. Don't you see? He was a fornicator. Don't you understand? I couldn't bear to see what Mikey had become over the years. Once so innocent . . . and then just as filthy as anyone, as filthy as all of us, a filthy and callow fornicator. Seeing what he became . . . in a way that soiled me, soiled the memories of what we'd once had. You can understand that.'

'No.'

'It soiled me,' Linski repeated, his voice gradually growing softer. He seemed lost and far away. 'Soiled me.'

'And what you did with him . . . that wasn't sin, wasn't filthy?'

'No.'

'Then what?'

'Love.'

War was waged to make peace. Abuse was love. Welcome to the funhouse, where strange mirrors reflect the faces of Hell.

Ben said, 'Would you have killed the girl with him?'

'Yes. If I'd had time. But you interrupted. And then . . . I just didn't care about her so much any more.'

'She was a witness. If she'd seen anything . . .' Linski shrugged.

'All your anger turned toward me.'

'You being a hero,' Judge said cryptically.

'What?'

'You being the war hero . . . what did that make me?'

'I don't know. What did it make you?'

'The villain, the monster,' he said, and tears welled in his eyes. 'Until you showed up, I was clean. I was judgment. Just passing judgment. But you're the big hero . . . and every hero has to have a monster to slay. So they made me the monster.'

Ben said nothing.

'I was only trying to preserve the memory of Mikey the way he was so long ago. The pure innocence that he was. Preserve it. Is that so bad?'

Finally, Linski sobbed.

Ben could not bear the weeping.

The killer huddled pathetically in the chair, trying to lift his taped hands so he could bury his face in them.

The trial. The press. Unending publicity. Back into the attic room to escape. And Linski, huddled and pathetic, would never spend time in a prison. A mental hospital, yes, but not prison. Innocent by reason of insanity.

He put one hand on Linski's head, smoothed his hair.

Linski leaned into the comforting touch.

'Everybody's damaged,' Chase said.

Linski looked up at him through tears.

'Some are just damaged too much. Far too much.'

'I'm sorry,' Linski said.

'It's okay.'

'I'm sorry.'

'Open wide for me.'

Linski knew what was coming. He opened his mouth.

Ben put the muzzle between Linski's teeth and pulled the trigger.

He dropped the gun and turned away from the dead man, walked into the hall, and opened the bathroom door. He put up the lid of the toilet bowl, dropped to his knees, and vomited. He remained on his knees for a long time before he could control the spasms that racked him. He flushed the toilet three times. He put the lid down and sat on it, blotting the cold sweat on his face with his gloved hands.

Having won the Congressional Medal of Honor, the most sacred and jealously guarded award his country bestowed, he had wanted nothing more than to return to the attic room in Mrs. Fielding's house and resume his penitence.

Then he met Glenda, and things changed. There was no question about living as a hermit any more, sealed off from experience. All that he wanted now was quietude, a chance for their love to develop, a life. Fauvel, the police, the press, and Richard Linski had not allowed him even that.

Chase rose and went to the sink. He rinsed his mouth out until the bad taste was gone.

He no longer had to be a hero.

He left the bathroom.

In the kitchen, he unwound the tape from Richard Linski's wrists and ankles. He let the body slide out of the chair and sprawl onto the floor.

When he considered the pistol, he realized that there would be three slugs missing from the clip. In the den he found a gun cabinet and drawers of ammunition. He reloaded the clip, leaving out only one round. In the kitchen, he put the gun on the floor, near the dead man's right hand.

In the living room, he searched for the two slugs that Judge had expended earlier. He found the one that had passed through his shoulder; it was embedded in the baseboard, and he dug it out without leaving a particularly noticeable mark. The other was on the floor behind the portable bar, where it had fallen after striking the bronze frame of the shattered bar mirror.

It was a quarter of twelve when he reached the Mustang and put the garbage bag and the cotton gloves into the trunk.

He drove past Linski's bungalow. The lights were on. They would burn all night.

* * *

Ben knocked twice, and Glenda let him into the motel room.

They held each other for a while.

'You're hurt.' When she realized the nature of the wound, she said, 'I'd better get you back to my place. You'll stay with me. I'll have to nurse you through this. We can't risk infection. Doctors have to report gunshot wounds to the police.'

She drove the Mustang.

He slumped in the passenger seat. A great weariness overcame him – not merely a result of the experiences of the past couple of hours but a weariness of years.

Heroes need monsters to slay, and they can

always find them – within if not without.

'You haven't asked,' he said as they rolled through the night.

'I never will.'

'He's dead.'

She said nothing.

'I think it was the right thing.'

'It was a door you had to go through, whether you wanted to or not,' she said.

'Only the Karneses can connect me to him, and they're never going to talk. The cops can't nail me for it.'

'Anyway,' she said, 'you'll make your own punishment.'

A full moon rode the night sky. He stared at its cratered face, trying to read the future in the destruction of the past.

DEAN KOONTZ

THE HOUSE OF THUNDER

In a cavern called The House of Thunder, Susan Thorton watched in terror as her lover died a brutal death in a college hazing. And in the following four years, the four young men who participated in that grim fraternity rite likewise died violently. Or did they?

Twelve years later Susan wakes in a hospital bed. Apparently involved in a fatal accident, she is suffering from amnesia. She doesn't remember who she is or why she is there. All she knows is that her convalescence is unfolding into a fearful nightmare – and that the faces that surround her, pretending loving care, are those of the four men involved in that murder years before.

Have the dead come back to life? Or has Susan plunged into the abyss of madness? With the help of her neurosurgeon, Susan desperately clings to her sanity while fighting to uncover who or what could be stalking her . . .

FICTION / GENERAL 0 7472 3661 5